ROARING BROOK PRESS

New York

THE
WORM WHIC

THE WORM WHISPERER

BETTY HICKS

ILLUSTRATED BY
BEN HATKE

In memory of my friend,
Lisa M. Thalhimer

Text copyright © 2013 by Betty Hicks
Illustrations copyright © 2013 by Ben Hatke
Published by Roaring Brook Press
Roaring Brook Press is a division of Holtzbrinck Publishing Holdings Limited Partnership
175 Fifth Avenue, New York, New York 10010
mackids.com

Library of Congress Cataloging-in-Publication Data

Hicks, Betty.
   The worm whisperer / Betty Hicks ; illustrated by Ben Hatke. — 1st ed.
      p. cm.
   Summary: Ellison Ellis Coffey, a lonely fifth-grader, discovers he might have the special gift of talking to bugs and decides to use his ability to win his town's annual Woolly Worm Race.
   ISBN 978-1-59643-490-5 (hardcover)—ISBN 978-1-59643-846-0 (ebook)
   [1. Worms—Fiction.   2. Insects—Fiction.   3. Human-animal communication—Fiction.   4. Racing—Fiction.]   I. Hatke, Ben, Ill.   II. Title.
   PZ7.H53155Wo 2012
   [Fic]—dc23

                                                                      2012013790

Roaring Brook Press books are available for special promotions and premiums.
For details contact: Director of Special Markets, Holtzbrinck Publishers.

First edition, 2013
Book design by Roberta Pressel
Printed in the United States of America by RR Donnelley & Sons Company, Harrisonburg, Virginia

10 9 8 7 6 5 4 3 2 1

CONTENTS

1   I'M NOT DEAD

Ellis liked everything about his obituary, even if it wasn't true.

An obituary is what gets written when you die. It's printed in the newspaper and says nice things—like how you've gone to heaven and how the world's a better place because you'd lived in it. Even if that's a lie, Ellis thought it was okay, because nobody wants to say bad things about a dead person.

He watched the minute hand on the classroom clock tick closer to three o'clock. Then he folded his obituary in half and slipped it into his book bag. For an obituary, it sounded pretty nice, but still . . . it had a lot of mistakes in it.

For one thing, thought Ellis, I'm not dead. Even though, just last week, he'd said, "I am *so* dead." That's because he accidentally ripped a hole in his mother's favorite quilt—the one hand-stitched by his great-great-great-grandmother Hattie May, who'd been dead almost as long as Moses.

Besides the quilt, Hattie May had handed down the best recipe for boiled custard on the planet. Ellis's grandmother still knew the secret for making it sweet, but not too sweet, melt in your mouth, perfect.

Ellis missed Gram's custard. Two months ago she and Pops had zipped straight out of Banner Elk behind the wheel of their dream RV, and Ellis had no idea when they'd be back. But they'd mailed him lots of picture postcards because they knew he loved animals. They sent alligators from Florida, coyotes from New Mexico, moose from Maine. He pinned them to the corkboard on the wall in his bedroom.

He'd also watched a million nature programs with his dad before television went digital. Now, their old TV—the one with antennae that stuck up like rabbit ears—was as extinct as a dinosaur. Luckily for Ellis, he could hike the half mile to his pond to watch wildlife there. He went every chance he got.

And, he read every animal or insect library book he could get his hands on. Mr. Turnmire, Ellis's teacher, said that Ellis was animal-obsessed.

Ellis thought that Mr. Turnmire was word-obsessed. He wrote a new vocabulary word on the board every day. Each word had to have at least four syllables and ten letters or Mr. Turnmire said it wasn't worthy of their fourth-grade brain power. Mr. Turnmire also claimed that a person with a good vocabulary could achieve anything.

Ellis was pretty sure that wasn't true. Fancy words couldn't fix his dad's back. Or get his mom's old job back. Or buy a new TV that worked.

The school clock ticked another minute closer to three.

Still . . . Ellis had to admit, Mr. Turnmire had an awesome dictionary. It was the size of a kitchen sink and weighed more than a baby pig. Every time Mr. Turnmire opened it, he promised, "Meaning and magnitude await!"

Mr. Turnmire was right. Fun words leaped out of it like small miracles. Ellis learned *injudicious*—a spectacular way to say "stupid." And *regurgitation*—a stupendous way to say "vomit."

Today's word had been *obituary*. That's how Ellis's obituary had gotten written before he was dead. It was part of an in-class assignment.

Molly had raised her hand and objected. "But Mr. Turnmire, *obituary* only has eight letters."

"Ah, but it has *five* syllables," Mr. Turnmire replied.

"That's good enough to override the ten-letter requirement—just for today. Never take yourself so seriously that you can't make exceptions to your own rules."

Ellis shot up in his seat. "I've got one!"

Mr. Turnmire lowered his head at Ellis and said, "Ellison Coffey. Please raise your hand when you have something to share."

"Sorry," Ellis apologized, and raised his hand.

"Yes?" said Mr. Turnmire.

"I've got one," Ellis repeated.

"You've got one what?"

"An exception to a rule."

Ellis could tell by the way Mr. Turnmire raised one eyebrow that he didn't want to hear what was coming next, but he nodded for Ellis to speak.

Ellis cleared his throat, paused for suspense, and said, "Exterminate homework."

The class cheered.

Ellis's chest puffed out—*exterminate* was one of last week's vocabulary words, and he'd made the class cheer.

"Exterminate?" asked Mr. Turnmire.

"It means get rid of," said Ellis.

"I know what it means," said Mr. Turnmire.

Ellis knew that homework was probably here to stay,

but it never hurt to ask. Without homework, he'd have more time at the pond to watch for ducks, foxes, groundhogs, deer, turkey—last week he'd seen a bobcat.

And, with no homework, he'd have more time to help his parents.

"No homework?" asked Mr. Turnmire, stroking his chin. "Not ever?"

"Well," said Ellis, trying his best to sound convincing. "Just no homework on days that end with the letter *y*."

Mr. Turnmire snorted. The class was quiet. Ellis could practically hear them naming the days of the week inside their heads: Monday . . . Tuesday . . . . Finally, they laughed.

"Nice try, Ellis," said Mr. Turnmire. "No homework?" He shook his head. "No way. But you get an A for effort. Way to use your brain!"

Ellis glanced around to see if everybody had heard Mr. Turnmire compliment his brain. Some pumped their fists. Others rolled their eyes. Randy gagged.

Alice was writing *obituary* in her vocabulary notebook. Ellis thought her hair was the exact same color as honey.

"Who'd like to use the word *obituary* in a sentence?" asked Mr. Turnmire.

Ellis searched his brain for a funny sentence. But there was nothing funny about death, so he burped.

The class laughed. Alice kept writing.

Mr. Turnmire sighed. "That'll do, Ellis."

Randy waved his hand in the air and said, "I have a sentence: 'Since Ellis is *so* dead, can I write his obituary'?"

"Hmm," said Mr. Turnmire. "Good idea."

Ellis's heart skipped a beat. Did Mr. Turnmire want him dead?

"I want you all to write each other's obituaries." Mr. Turnmire paused and thought a minute. "You'll draw names. Each of you will write the obituary of the classmate

whose name you draw. But remember"—he raised one finger into the air—"obituaries honor a person. All your comments must be kind."

While Mr. Turnmire collected everyone's names on slips of paper, Ellis looked around the room and wondered whose name he'd get. He didn't know enough about anybody there to sum up a whole life.

Molly was picky and sometimes bossy . . . but nice. George was fun, had big ears, and his dad had a CB radio in his truck. Alice was quiet, except when Randy bullied somebody or stomped on innocent ants, and then she'd shout, "Stop!" She had shiny hair, got good grades, and twice she'd checked out the same library book as Ellis. He thought that meant she liked animals and insects just like he did. And Randy . . . well, Randy was a jerk.

Ellis drew a name out of the basket as Mr. Turnmire passed it. He unfolded the paper and read, "Randy." He reached out, trying to put it back, but Mr. Turnmire had already moved up the row to the next desk.

What could he write about Randy? *Bully? Pea brain? Stink breath?*

After a lot of thinking that made his head hurt, Ellis wrote:

Randy sang in the church choir. He liked playing tag at recess and was dearly beloved by his mother, his father, and his dog.

Ellis ended with a big fat lie and wrote,

He will be missed by everyone.

George drew Ellis's name. He wrote:

Ellison "Ellis" Coffey lived his whole happy life in Banner Elk, North Carolina. His family ran a blueberry farm, and that's why Ellis's fingertips looked like ink. He loved animals and insects. He was very funny and had lots of friends. Mr. Turn-mire called him our class-clown-but-with-brains. The world was a better place because Ellis lived in it.

Ellis wished it were true.

He *had* lived his whole life in Banner Elk. He *was* funny. He did love animals. And he picked a lot of blue-berries. Sometimes he squeezed them too hard, so his fingertips got inky-looking. But George was wrong about everything else. Ellis's life wasn't all that happy. He didn't have friends—just people who thought he was funny. It wasn't the same thing. And the world was not a better place because he lived in it.

The minute hand ticked straight up to three o'clock. Ellis slung his book bag over one shoulder. Time to go home. He wished he didn't have to.

2 THE SPIDER DANCE

Ellis climbed onto the school bus.

"Hey, Ellis," yelled George. "Come to the park."

"Can't." Ellis shouted back. He was surprised George didn't know that by now.

Ellis never hung out at the park after school. If he missed the bus, he'd have no way home. He lived too far out to catch a ride with anyone.

Plus, he had things to do at home. He had floors to sweep, laundry to fold, homework to do, Dad to look after.

Ellis slid into a seat behind two second-grade girls. He slipped a piece of paper out of his book bag and tore it into small pieces. Then he rolled one of the pieces of paper into a ball and tossed it between the girls. They stopped talking and turned. Ellis pretended to read his library book, *All About Ants*.

As soon as they turned back around, Ellis lobbed another paper ball, then leaned back in his seat and read his
book again, as if he'd never looked up. The girls giggled.

The third time, they turned around just as he was getting ready to throw. "We caught you!" they squealed. Then
they hid their heads. They couldn't stop giggling.

Second graders are easy, thought Ellis. He could make
them laugh with one hand tied behind his back.

Ellis hadn't always been funny. He used to be quiet, like
his dad. And his granddad. Coffey men didn't say much.

But last spring, something happened. Ellis's class went
on a field trip. Not the kind where you go to a museum
and touch dinosaur bones, or to a cave and see bat drop-
pings. This was a field trip *to a field*—Mrs. Puckett's corn-
field. His science teacher, Miss Williams, wanted the class
to see how many different kinds of insects they could find.

Ellis couldn't wait. He ran ahead of everyone, tromping
through giant weeds and tall, dead cornstalks. Then, all
of a sudden, sticky stuff covered his face. Tiny legs crawled
over one ear and across his eyes and into his nose. Ellis
had plunged his face into the biggest spiderweb in Avery
County.

He went crazy. He waved his arms and jumped up and
down. He stuck his fingers up his nose to get rid of

whatever was creeping around in there. He swiped his eyes and pulled away wispy stuff.

"Look at Ellis!" someone yelled.

"He's funny," shouted somebody else.

Ellis looked around. Everyone was laughing. Not *at* him. No. They were joining him, waving their arms and imitating him as if he'd invented the world's funniest dance—the spider dance. They pulled at their hair and flung their bodies like rag dolls between the corn rows.

Ellis tried to explain about the spiderweb, but they were all having too much fun to listen.

Suddenly, Ellis felt different. Changed somehow. Almost as if he'd discovered some new power. It made him feel all tingly inside. Even the top of his head tingled.

No. Wait.

That wasn't his head that was tingling. Something was actually moving in his hair.

Ellis reached up and plucked a wiggly creature off the top of his head and dangled it by one long, thin leg.

"Yikes!" exclaimed Molly. "That's a spider!"

"It's just a daddy longlegs," said Alice. She walked over carrying a small box in her hands with three insects in it that she'd found. "It won't hurt you."

Ellis looked at the insect dangling from his fingers. He wondered if Alice had missed his spider dance.

His insides were still tingly from making everyone laugh and dance funny. He glanced around. All his classmates were watching. He lowered the spider over his open mouth and acted as if he were going to swallow it.

Choruses of "eeew" and "nasty" and "yuck" rang out around him, followed by hoots of laughter.

"Do it!" cheered Randy.

"Don't," said Alice.

The spider swiveled away from Ellis's mouth. Panicked, it twitched in the empty air.

Ellis listened to the laughter. It felt good.

But then he sensed something else. Fear. The spider was freaking out. Anyone could see that, but Ellis actually felt tiny needles of adrenaline pricking his insides.

Carefully, he placed the spider on the ground and watched it scurry to safety under a cornstalk.

"Wimp," jeered Randy.

"Thanks," said Alice.

Ellis's scared-spider feeling faded away. For a second he wondered where it had come from. But then everyone was telling him what a riot he was. He shrugged and tried to act as if it were no big deal. But on the inside, he was grinning like crazy.

From then on, he knew he had a reputation to uphold— class funny kid. He cracked people up.

And he was good at it. Right now, the second-grade girls in front of him on the bus were still giggling.

Ellis rested the side of his head against the window and counted, one by one, the telephone poles that whipped past. He wondered if Alice and Molly had gone to the park with George. He wondered for about the millionth time if Alice actually *liked* spiders. If he gave her one, would she thank him?

Tired of telephone poles, Ellis began to count mail-boxes. At Macky Road, seven kids got off his bus. After two more mailboxes, five kids hopped off, including the giggling girls. More mailboxes. More kids. Finally, Ellis was the only one left—Ellis and Mr. V, the bus driver.

They rode five more minutes with *no* mailboxes— nothing to see but blueberry bushes. Most of them belonged to Ellis's family. Their blueberry farm went back even farther in time than Hattie May's quilt.

The bus turned off onto a dirt road and began to climb the mountain. Ellis had to move his head away from the windowpane because it was bumping his brains into marbles.

Four more curves.

"End of the line," Mr. V called to Ellis. The bus squeaked to a stop in front of his rutted driveway. Mr. V pushed the lever that opened the door. "How's your dad?" he asked.

"Fine," Ellis lied.

"You tell your mom I got extra tomatoes going to waste. She's welcome to pick some, but she'll have to hurry. First hard freeze'll get them soon."

"Thanks," said Ellis. He climbed down off the bus.

Ellis hiked up and around one more curve before his house came into view. It was an old white farmhouse that had a wraparound porch with ferns hanging on it. The plants were a sick green color that meant he needed to water them.

But first, he needed to check on Dad.

3 FAKING FUNNY

Ellis banged in through the kitchen, letting the screen door slam behind him. Mom's "Trust in the Lord" cross-stitch sampler slid sideways.

"That you, son?" called Dad.

"No," joked Ellis. "Escaped convict."

"Armed?" asked Dad.

"And dangerous!" Ellis growled in his best wanted-for-murder voice. He lunged into the living room, swinging his book bag as if he were David, about to hurl rocks at Goliath.

Dad laughed, held up his hands, and surrendered. He was lying as close to flat as he could get in a La-Z-Boy recliner.

He *had* to lie flat. He had a herniated disk in his back that made sitting hurt worse than a toothache the size of

Beech Mountain. Standing hurt even more. And house painting, which was his job, was impossible. He hadn't painted anything in months.

The first time Ellis heard "herniated disk," he'd thought it was a new kind of CD or DVD. But it wasn't. It had something to do with not having enough squishy stuff between the stacked-up bones in your spine. Fixing it meant surgery. Surgery meant paying a deductible.

Deductible, thought Ellis. Four syllables and ten letters. A word Mr. Turnmire would love. It meant health insurance wouldn't pay for all the surgery. His dad would have to pay the first thousand dollars of it.

Only they didn't have a thousand dollars.

Dad tapped his crossword puzzle book with a pencil. He wore jeans, a T-shirt, and brown leather boots so old they were scuffed almost white. For years, Mom had tried to get him to buy new ones, but he loved those boots. "I like what I got," he'd say.

Ellis hoped that one day he'd look like his dad: tall, with a lot of muscles. But lately, Ellis thought that pain had shrunk him.

"What's an eight-letter word for *impossible*?" asked Dad.

"*Surgery*?" answered Ellis.

"Not enough letters," Dad muttered.

"Dad," groaned Ellis, "I was being funny."

"Oh." Dad nodded. "Right."

"Dad?"

"Hmmm?"

"If Mom liked spiders, would you give her one?"

Dad tilted his head back and thought about it. He took weird questions seriously. But sometimes he took forever to answer them.

Ellis shifted his weight from one side to another. He wiggled his fingers. He waited.

"I'd give her a ladybug," Dad finally answered.

"Not a spider?"

Dad shook his head. "Nope."

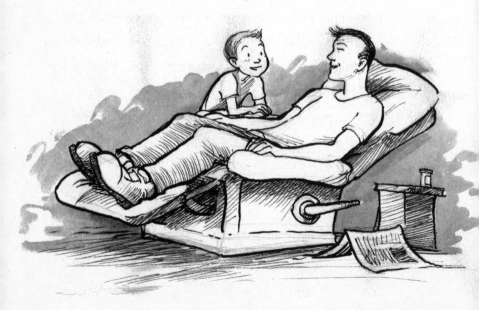

"What about an ant farm?" Alice hated for Randy to stomp on ants.

"Your mother hates ants."

"What if it's not for Mom? What if it's for somebody else?"

"Who?"

"Uh, I dunno . . . nobody."

"A girl?"

"Yeah."

"She pretty?" Dad raised his eyebrows.

"*Dad*," Ellis said with a groan.

"Beware of pretty girls." Dad shook his head solemnly, as if he were warning Ellis to keep away from nuclear waste.

"Huh?"

"Sometimes they don't turn out as great as you think."

"Wasn't Mom pretty?"

"Still is," said Dad. He gave his head a quick, sure jerk, as if it was the only thing in life he knew for a fact.

"So," asked Ellis, "are you saying Mom's not as great as you thought?"

Dad choked. He coughed and gagged so much, Ellis wondered if he'd have to pound on his bad back. He hoped not.

Dad finally stopped coughing and cleared his throat. When he leaned forward to get up, he stopped midway. His jaw clenched, but he made his face stay normal. Dad didn't like to show pain, but Ellis could see it in his eyes. When he felt good, his eyes danced around a lot. When he hurt, they just sat frozen in their sockets, like a statue's.

He reminded Ellis of Superman—one part mild-mannered Clark Kent, a quiet guy who worked crossword puzzles and watched nature TV. And one part strong man—who never showed pain and could leap tall buildings in a single bound or stare down a grizzly bear if he had to.

Ellis remembered the time Dad saved him from a rattlesnake. They were hiking and Ellis had bent down to tie his bootlace. He was face-to-face with a rattler, one foot away and ready to strike. Out of nowhere, Dad had stepped between them and intercepted the bite and the venom. The bite pierced Dad's pants. He was sick for days.

How do you thank a dad who does that? Every time he'd tried, Dad just shrugged. "No big deal."

"Do you want your pain pills?" asked Ellis.

"Not time yet," Dad whispered.

"Something to eat?"

"No thanks."

"Ten million dollars?"

Dad forced a laugh, but it came out fake. He gave up trying to stand, sank back into his recliner, and closed his statue eyes.

Ellis went into the utility room off the kitchen. Shoved into one corner sat all the equipment for things Dad didn't do anymore: his hiking boots, his fly rod for trout fishing, a kayak paddle.

On top of the dryer sat a mound of clean clothes. Ellis plucked a T-shirt off the top of the pile. It had a blueberry stain that never came out, not even with bleach. Ellis folded it into a square. Well . . . sort of a square. Close enough. He wondered where the best place to find a ladybug might be.

When all the clothes were folded, he went back into the kitchen to wash the dirty dishes soaking in the sink. He picked up Mom's Bible that she'd left open on the counter and moved it to a table where it wouldn't get wet. Then he felt around underwater for a plate and sponged it off.

Ellis gazed out the window. Something orange twitched—a tail. Ginger, the stray cat that hung around their house, stalked a chipmunk in the ivy under the maple tree.

Ellis used to feed the strays that passed through, but Mom made him quit.

"It's all we can do to feed ourselves," she'd said.

It was true. Since Mom had lost her job and Dad couldn't work, they ate a lot of cheap stuff—potatoes, bread, noodles. But still . . . Ellis didn't see why he couldn't occasionally feed one skinny cat.

Ellis figured Mom was just tired and extra crabby because, when she'd worked for the phone company, she'd gotten home at three o'clock. Then the economy crashed or fell apart or something, and she'd been laid off.

Now, mornings, she cleaned houses for the rich people who lived on the golf course. Lunchtime, she drove around digging through dumpsters, looking for junk that Dad could fix up and sell. Afternoons and nights, she waited tables at Pappy's Barbeque. Really late at night, she made blueberry muffins, pies, and jam to sell at the farmer's market.

Ellis barely ever saw her.

He stacked the clean dishes in the drain board and sponged off the kitchen table that had a dozen cracks in its Formica top. Then he dried his hands on an old worn dish towel and went to check on Dad.

He was snoring, making funny little sputtering sounds like a motorboat.

Good, thought Ellis. He smiled.

He returned to the kitchen and searched the cabinets for duck food to take to the pond. He grabbed two fistfuls of Cheerios and stuffed them into his pockets. Then he straightened Mom's "Trust in the Lord" wall hanging.

He'd already trusted in the Lord. He'd prayed every day for Dad to be fixed, and for Mom to get her old job back, but it hadn't worked.

Maybe he should pray for something easier. Like an afternoon at the park.

"Please, God," he said. "Let me stay just one measly day after school and—"

No. He stopped. He didn't want to use up a perfectly good prayer on something that couldn't last.

4 🐛 I'M A ROCK

"We're going on a ladybug hunt," Ellis sang as he walked through the trees on the path to the pond.

He stopped and drew in a breath so deep his chest puffed out. He could actually taste the fall leaves in the air—earthy and crisp. They shaded the narrow wooded path with a bright roof of yellow, red, and orange. As dozens fell and swirled around him, Ellis felt as if he were being bathed in a box of crayons.

He gazed uphill. If he climbed the hundred feet to the top he could see the Smokey Mountains and a trillion more colored leaves stretching all the way to Tennessee. It was his mother's favorite place, especially in October. He wondered if she'd even noticed the leaves this year.

Ellis hiked down instead—toward the pond. He'd rather feed ducks. And talk to them.

Ellis grew quiet and walked as if he were part of the mountain—with super soft footfalls. Then he whispered under his breath, "Here, Socks. Here, Scar." That's what he'd named the foxes he sometimes caught a glimpse of. Socks had black legs that looked as if he were wearing knee socks. Scar had a place on his face that looked like something had bitten him.

In spite of his stealth, they were nowhere in sight. But Puddle and her ducklings spotted Ellis as soon as he stepped into the clearing. Puddle is what he'd named the mother mallard. All of them glided toward him, leaving one big V wave and eleven little tiny ones behind them in the flat water.

"Hi guys," Ellis called out. "Where's your dad?"

Ellis hadn't seen the daddy duck in weeks. Was he hurt? Did ducks get herniated disks?

Eleven baby ducks spurted forward.

"Chow time," said Ellis. He pulled out the Cheerios and flung some into the water.

The ducks went bottoms up, tipping their beaks into the water. Puddles held back, letting her chicks have all the food.

"Today, I cracked a lot of people up," he told them. "I had them practically rolling in the aisles." Ellis tucked his hands under his arms and waddled like a duck. "What do you think?"

The ducks lifted their heads, watching.

"Well . . . not Alice, but everybody else. Have you guys seen any ladybugs?"

All twelve ducks fixed their eyes on Ellis.

"I even made Dad laugh for about two seconds. And Mr. Turnmire complimented my brain. But I had to write Randy's obituary, and it had to be nice. That was harder than trying to spell dinosaur names."

The ducks watched and listened.

"Anybody still hungry?"

All twelve ducks splashed their wings impatiently.

"Okay," said Ellis. He smiled and tossed them more cereal.

Then Ellis dropped to his knees. He spent the next twenty minutes crawling around, separating every blade of grass that grew near the pond, looking for a ladybug.

Nothing. Maybe, if he was quiet, one would come to him. He inched a few feet back into the woods and sat cross-legged on his rock. He wiggled his butt around until it fit the groove. He slowed his breathing. He imagined himself as part of the rock.

Invisible, he waited.

Ellis heard a twig snap across the pond. A deer stepped out of the woods, her nose high in the air, sniffing. She was no more than a stone's throw from where he sat.

Ellis hoped he wasn't upwind. He watched the bright colored leaves on the trees ripple toward him. Good—he was downwind. The deer wouldn't pick up his scent. But still . . . her ears could hear a feather fall. Dad told him that when a leaf falls in the forest, an eagle can see it, a bear can smell it, and a deer can hear it.

Ellis held his breath.

Cautiously, the doe lowered her head to drink. Ellis exhaled slowly and shifted his weight. The deer's head jerked up. She stared straight at Ellis.

Ellis felt her fear. It was like the day he'd felt the

spider's panic, only this was bigger. He actually felt the deer's own heartbeat pounding in his chest.

Her eyes were locked on Ellis's.

Enemy? they asked.

Ellis held her gaze. He guided his breath in with a deep controlled inhale. Then he let it out—long and slow—and whispered, "Friend."

With his voice, his eyes, and his heart, he sent the word and its meaning across the small pond.

The doe lowered her head and went back to drinking.

Ellis's whole body tingled with excitement.

He could be a deer whisperer.

Just like Mrs. Puckett.

Mrs. Puckett was the woman who had let his class take a field trip to her field. Small, white-haired, and wrinkled, she oozed ancient wisdom vibes. That's because Mrs. Puckett was a horse whisperer. When she spoke, horses listened.

The day he'd invented the spider dance, his class had stopped by her farmhouse to thank her for letting a bunch of kids stomp around looking for insects. Her farmhand said she was busy stabling a fractious horse. He invited them to pet the goats while they waited.

Ellis didn't know what *fractious* meant, but it sounded interesting. While everyone else was busy petting goats, he slipped around the side of the barn. He wanted to see the horse.

Mrs. Puckett was skinnier than a stick of straw but she stood in front of the stable door, tugging on the reins of a shiny, ink-black horse that didn't want to budge. Suddenly the huge horse reared up with his ears back flat and pawed the air like he wanted to pound poor Mrs. Puckett into dust balls.

She didn't appear any bigger than a raindrop compared to the size of that horse, but she stood as calm as a lake. She looked the beast straight in both eyes and whispered. Ellis couldn't hear the words, but he felt them. They were peaceful, and they had a slow rhythm, like a lullaby. But they had a firmness, too. The air around those words felt so enchanted, it pricked up the hairs on the back of his neck.

The horse stopped rearing, but he still pranced, and his ears twitched. Mrs. Puckett looked him in both eyes, stroked his neck with her fingers, and kept on whispering.

Slowly . . . slowly, the horse settled. He blew a gentle puff of air through his nostrils. Then he lowered his head and nuzzled the palm of Mrs. Puckett's hand.

Ellis understood. He had felt the words too.

Even more amazing, he knew what the horse felt. Rage. It had filled the air with flashes of light and heat as real as lightning bolts. Then Mrs. Puckett's words had reduced them to beams of light that flickered, then dimmed, and finally died, replaced by a soft glow. It had been incredible.

And now Ellis was experiencing the same thing with the deer. He felt his muscles relax with hers. The sparks of tension that had filled the air with her fear vanished as if they'd fallen into the pond and been snuffed out by the rippling water.

Ellis felt as magical as Mrs. Puckett.

He sat on his rock and watched the deer drink. And the ducks swim. A groundhog poked its whiskers out of a crevice in some rocks.

That's when he saw the woolly worm crawling over his foot.

"Chester?"

It looked exactly like Chester, but—no way. Ellis had released him back into the woods a year ago—right after last year's Woolly Worm Race.

"Do I know you?" asked Ellis.

The caterpillar kept on crawling until he disappeared over the side of the rock.

"You can't be Chester," Ellis called after him. "You would've turned into a butterfly by now." Ellis didn't understand why they were called worms, because they were really caterpillars.

Last year, he'd entered a woolly worm in the annual race at the Banner Elk Woolly Worm Festival. He'd named him Chester and had been convinced that he was a winner because he never quit moving the entire time Ellis held him.

But when the race started and the other contestants zipped straight up their strings toward the finish line, Chester planted his gazillion tiny feet and stopped. He never moved again. Not an inch.

Maybe he'd give Alice a woolly worm—one she could race. Or even better, he'd get one that *he* could race. When he won, she'd congratulate him. Then he'd give it to her, and they'd walk to the park to release it.

Ellis watched two more woolly worms inch across his rock.

"My name's Ellis," he whispered.

The worms sped up.

"You guys are fast. You should race," said Ellis.

The caterpillars ignored him.

"I'm serious," Ellis persisted. He hoped he was using his whispering voice. He scrambled off the rock and stretched flat on his belly in the leaves so he could make eye contact.

He looked straight into a pair of black beady eyes and whispered, "Twenty thousand people come here just to race worms . . . or to watch. All you have to do is sprint up a string faster than anybody else and you win."

The other caterpillar continued to crawl away. But the one Ellis had locked eyes with stopped and lifted its head. Maybe Ellis was imagining it, but he could swear the caterpillar's head tilt asked, Win what?

It was like the spider and the deer. Ellis wasn't just reading body language, he knew what it felt—this caterpillar was curious.

Ellis kept talking. "The winner forecasts the weather for the whole winter. You don't actually talk, of course. You're just a caterpillar."

The woolly worm bristled.

"No offense," said Ellis.

Its spiky fuzz relaxed a little.

Ellis pointed to the caterpillar's black and brown stripes. "The mayor reads your thirteen bands of color. Each one of those stands for a different week of winter."

The wooly worm twisted his head to study its own body—thirteen bands, the first two dark, followed by nine lighter reddish brown ones, then two more dark.

Ellis took a deep breath and tried to stay focused. He

pointed to the second band that was so dark it was black. "See," he said slowly, "that dark one is week number two. If you win, it means we'll get a blizzard that week." He pointed to the lightest-colored band near the middle. "That week the weather'll be warm enough to pack a picnic and go to the park."

The worm shrugged.

Well, Ellis guessed it was a shrug. It was a tiny ripple where the worm's shoulders would be—if a worm had shoulders.

The woolly worm put its head down and went back to crawling.

"Wait!" cried Ellis, losing his calm. "The winning worm wins a thousand dollars!"

The caterpillar continued to inch away.

"One . . . thousand . . . dollars." Ellis repeated slowly to himself.

Suddenly, Ellis knew exactly how to help his dad.

5 CATERPILLAR CASTLE

"All you have to do," said Ellis, leaning forward to pick up the woolly worm, "is win one measly little race."

That wasn't exactly true. The caterpillar would have to win three races—a heat, one semifinal, and the final race. But Ellis didn't want to scare him with too many details.

The odds were tough enough—dozens of heats with twenty-five caterpillars in each one. That equaled what? A thousand? Two thousand worms? Ellis didn't have any idea, except that there'd be a *lot* of woolly worms this little guy would have to beat.

But the most important number was one thousand. That's how much money they'd win. The exact same amount as Dad's deductible.

Ellis looked down at his winning worm. It had rolled up into a ball in his hand and was playing dead.

"Hey," cried Ellis. "You're a racer! Wake up!"

The caterpillar curled tighter.

Oh, man, thought Ellis. A minute ago he had connected with this caterpillar. He'd been exactly like Mrs. Puckett and her horse whispering. Only he was a worm whisperer.

"Come on," he urged.

Ellis picked up the prickly ball and whispered into the area where its ear might be, "*Yooou* are in my power. *Yooou* must do what I say."

The woolly worm didn't budge.

Ellis had a feeling he sounded more like a hypnotist than a worm whisperer. He cleared his throat and tried again.

"I'm your friend. There's nothing to be afraid of." His voice was smooth, gentle, coaxing, as musical as a lullaby. "Stretch your legs. Crawl up my thumb. It'll be okay. Honest."

The caterpillar slowly uncurled and began exploring Ellis's thumb. Up one side and down the other.

Ellis let out a whoop.

The woolly worm froze.

"Sorry," Ellis whispered. "Don't worry. I'm going to take you home and make you the coziest place to live you ever saw."

He swept up some pine needles and dried leaves and stuffed them into his pocket. Then he grabbed two rocks—one extra smooth, the other covered in moss—and slid them into his other pocket. Last, he spotted a chunky stick that was wet and spongy, good for moisture.

"Puddle! Guys!" He called to his ducks. "I'm going to win a thousand dollars!" They flapped their wings like crazy, then settled back into the water.

"Thanks," said Ellis, taking a bow.

With the wood chunk in one hand and the woolly worm in the other, Ellis ran home. He pulled the screen door open so fast he almost tore it off its hinges.

"That you?" called Dad.

"Yeah." Out of breath, Ellis panted. "You okay?"

"Yep."

"Need anything?"

"Nope."

"I'll be in my room."

Ellis raced up to his room taking three steps at a time.

The first thing he needed to do was keep his promise and make a first-class caterpillar castle—a place where his woolly worm could live happily ever after. Or until October 16—the day of the Woolly Worm Race.

Wait. The first thing he needed to do was name his worm. Ellis looked at him . . . her?

He turned the caterpillar over and looked underneath. That's where you figured out if puppies and kittens were male or female.

No clue.

He whispered, "Nod your head if you're a guy."

It rolled up into a bushy circle in his palm again.

"Are you a girl?" Ellis asked.

The caterpillar uncurled and looked up at him. Its head bobbed up and down. Well, maybe not a bob exactly, but a tiny move, like a hiccup.

"You're a girl!"

Ellis began to list aloud every girl's name he could think of: "Alice, Molly, Hattie May? Ruth, Bathsheba, Wonder Woman?"

The caterpillar stared at him, waiting, as if she had faith that he would eventually say the perfect name

Animal names, thought Ellis. Who was in *The Jungle Book*? Baloo, Shere Khan, Bagheera—all guys.

Did the alligator in *Peter Pan* have a name? Ellis shook his head. It didn't have any girls, either—just pirates. And lost boys.

"Wait!" cried Ellis. "How about Wendy?"

The caterpillar seemed to shrink.

"Tinkerbell?" asked Ellis.

The caterpillar tilted her head. Ellis felt her interest.

"What about Tink—for short?"

The caterpillar bobbed her head twice.

Ellis grinned so wide he almost split a lip. He was going to win a thousand dollars for his dad! Not only that, he had a caterpillar to talk to.

He flung open his closet door and dug out an old shoe box. With a sharp pencil, he poked holes in the lid. Then he emptied his pockets into it—leaf litter, rocks, the spongy stick. Ellis arranged it all to look extra homey. Then he carefully placed Tink on the mossy rock and watched her disappear under it.

He wondered if that was good or bad. He wondered what he should feed her.

He knew that exotic lemurs from Madagascar ate fruit and leaves—except for the ones that ate only bamboo. And he knew that a giant peppered cockroach from Costa Rica will eat just about anything. But he had no idea what a woolly worm from Banner Elk ate. He'd found Chester right before last year's race and released him as soon as it was over. He'd never had to feed him.

Ellis turned his pockets inside out. A few broken Cheerios spilled out into the box. Tink didn't even give them a sniff. Maybe she was in shock. He wasn't getting any feelings from her. None at all.

He placed the lid on and hoped all she needed was a little privacy.

6 ▬▬ A PROMISE AND A PROBLEM

Downstairs, Ellis peeled potatoes for dinner over an open trash can.

Mom trudged in carrying an armload of new junk for Dad to fix up. She dumped it just inside the door.

"Hi, Ellie," she said, giving his hair a tousle. Her lips pecked the top of his head.

"Mom," said Ellis. "Ellie is a girl's name." The only thing worse was when she called him "Ellie baby." A girl *and* an infant.

"Hi, *Ellis,*" said Mom. She smiled at him as she moved past him on her way to check on Dad.

"Guess what I found?" Ellis called out to her.

No answer. Instead, he heard her asking Dad how his day had been.

"Great," answered Dad.

"Me, too," said Mom. Then they both laughed, probably because they both knew that they were lying.

Ellis waited a minute or two, listening to their low voices, then repeated, "Guess what I found?"

"Hmmm?" answered Mom, walking back into the kitchen, sifting through the mail. She looked tired.

"A woolly worm," said Ellis.

"That's nice." Mom swiped at a stubborn strand of hair that dangled in her face. She pulled an envelope out of the stack and frowned. Ellis recognized the church logo on it. That didn't make sense—church stuff always made her smile.

Mom sighed and put the church letter at the back of the stack. Then she flipped through the rest of the mail and pulled out a postcard. She handed it to Ellis. On the front he saw a giant Kodiak bear scooping a fish out of a waterfall. Ellis flipped the card over.

Ellis Honey,
  Hello from Alaska. We miss you so much! Pops caught a salmon yesterday—just like this bear, only Pops used a fishing pole.
                          Hug Yourself Twice!
                          Gram and Pops

Ellis read it three times. Then he examined the bear more closely. His claws were bigger than Ellis's foot. The fish was a sockeye salmon. He wondered if they ate plankton and squid like king salmon did. He hoped that Tink was upstairs chowing down on her Cheerios.

When he looked back up, Mom seemed different. Her whole body had slumped. Not a tired slump—she was always tired. This was something more. Ellis searched for a strong-enough word. Sorrowful.

The envelope with the church logo sat on the counter, torn open. Mom crumpled the letter she was holding and flung it into the trash can with the potato peels.

"What's wrong?" asked Ellis.

"Nothing," said Mom. She began putting dishes away, slowly stacking one on top of the other in the cabinet.

"Mom," said Ellis. "I just remembered. Mr. V told me he has extra tomatoes. You should stop and pick some before they freeze." He thought free food would cheer her up.

"Oh," said Mom, swiping at her loose hair strand again. "Well . . . that's kind of him, but I don't have anything to give him in return." She sagged against the counter. "I'm saving all our canned and frozen food for our booth at the Woolly Worm Festival."

"But, Mom, he's *giving* them away. He doesn't expect anything back."

"I know." Mom shrugged. "But I'd feel obliged—I hate to be beholden."

Ellis stared at her. He wanted to tell her that was crazy. This was free food. Besides, he loved tomato sandwiches. He liked to make them on soft bread slathered with mayonnaise.

"Okay," he muttered.

Mom sighed. She walked over and knelt in front of Ellis. She squeezed his thigh. "Ellie baby," she said in a voice that was even softer than Mrs. Puckett's. "I'm really sorry things are a little tough right now. But they'll get better. I just—" She paused, wiped two tears off her cheeks, stood, turned, and hurried out of the kitchen.

Ellis stared after her. Was she crying? Why? Because she couldn't give Mr. V anything in exchange for his tomatoes? Or something else?

What had the letter from church said?

Ellis reached down into the cold, wet pile of potato peels and fished out the soggy, crumpled letter. It was some kind of statement with a bunch of numbers on it—like a bill, but not a bill. It was a reminder—of a pledge.

Ellis dropped it back into the trash can.

It stated how much was still owed on the donation his mom and dad had promised to the church.

But that wasn't fair! They'd made that promise before Dad had had to quit work. Before Mom lost her job. This was the *church* for Pete's sake. It was *God. He* would understand if they didn't have the money. Wouldn't He?

"Bye, Frank," Ellis heard Mom call out to Dad.

"Got to run," she said to Ellis as she hurried back through the kitchen. She tried to sound cheerful, but her eyes were red and puffy. "Remember to label the jam jars. Don't stay up too late."

"Hey, Mom," said Ellis. "Look." He grabbed a spoon

and balanced it on his nose. She forced out a little fake laugh, and then she was gone.

Dad appeared in the doorway. Ellis could tell from the blank statue look that his pain pills had worn off again.

"What say we skip the potatoes?" said Dad.

"You sure?"

"Yeah."

Ellis made two cheese sandwiches. While he sliced the cheese, he thought about the pledge problem. And how Mom hated to be beholden. And then it hit him. It wasn't God. Or the church. It was his parents. A church pledge was a promise, and Mom and Dad never broke a promise.

No big deal, thought Ellis. I'm a worm whisperer. I can fix everything.

Ellis got out the bread and wondered how Tink was doing. What if she stayed under her rock and never came out? What if she died because he couldn't find anything she liked to eat? What if he *wasn't* a worm whisperer?

Ellis spread butter on the bread and thought about what he'd do if Tink didn't win. He'd need to make money some other way. Not enough for the church and definitely not a thousand dollars. But he could earn enough to buy cat food for strays and maybe a few tomatoes.

Ellis thought up ideas as he finished the sandwiches. Then he put them on plates and carried them into the living room where Dad was lying down. Ellis sank into a big soft armchair next to the empty TV stand. Dad leaned back in his recliner, balancing his sandwich plate on his stomach.

"Guess what I saw at the pond?" said Ellis.

"Hmm?" Dad answered.

"My ducks—all twelve of them—a deer, and a groundhog." He took a bite of his sandwich. "And a woolly worm that looked like Chester. Remember Chester?"

"Chester." Dad chuckled.

"Yeah," said Ellis. "The fast and fuzzy caterpillar that failed. He never moved."

"Barely an inch," said Dad.

They ate in silence for a while. Ellis didn't want to tell Dad his racing plans. He wanted it to be a surprise. Besides, he didn't want to get his hopes up and then lose.

Ellis thought some more about his other ideas to make money.

"Dad?" he asked.

Ellis's dad was still balancing his sandwich on his stomach. Every now and then he took a bite. "Um-hmm?"

"I've been thinking," said Ellis.

"Uh-oh."

"No, Dad. Seriously."

Dad studied Ellis's face. He nodded.

"I'd like to earn some money."

"Okay." He raised one eyebrow.

"I could mow lawns."

Dad thought and thought. Finally he said, "Whose?"

"I don't know. Neighbors."

"Son, our nearest neighbor is three miles away."

"Well," said Ellis. "I could have a paper route."

"Our nearest neighbor is three miles away," Dad repeated.

"A lemonade stand?"

"Son," said Dad. He looked tired, like Mom.

"I know," said Ellis. "Our nearest neighbor is three miles away."

"Ellis." Dad faked a smile that looked about as real as a car salesman's on TV. "Stop worrying. We're okay."

Ellis didn't want to call his dad a liar, so he took their plates to the kitchen and washed the dishes. After that he labeled the jam jars, and finally he went to check on Tink. She *had* to win the race.

Tink hadn't moved, and the Cheerios hadn't been nibbled.

Ellis whispered into the box, "What do you eat?"

Part of him believed she would crawl out from under her rock and tell him, "A leaf sundae with dirt and nuts."

Another part of him knew that caterpillars couldn't tell you what they thought, even with head bobs.

Ellis leaned closer to the box. "I *am* a worm whisperer," he said softly. "Right?"

Tink didn't answer.

7 🐛 WOOLLY WORM FOOD

Ellis rolled over in bed. He opened one eye. Daylight. It was morning. Saturday morning; a week away from the Woolly Worm Race.

Both eyes popped open.

Tink!

He bolted out of bed and ripped the lid off the shoe box. Tink was still under her rock. She hadn't touched a single Cheerio crumb.

"Ellis!" Dad called from downstairs. "Want to ride with me to the store?"

"Yes!" answered Ellis, surprised that Dad felt good enough to drive. Maybe someone at the store could tell him what to feed a woolly worm.

"Hang on," he whispered to Tink. "I'll be back. With food."

Ellis flew down the stairs, cleared the last three in one leap, and landed with a thud at the bottom. Dad was already on his way out the door.

Ellis followed him out and climbed up into his old Jeep—the one with a rusted-out hole in the floorboard and canvas flaps for windows. It was a classic—a 1979 CJ5—which didn't mean much to Ellis, but to his dad it was even better than a pet caterpillar.

"What are we going to the store for?" Ellis asked.

"Supplies."

What kind of supplies?"

"Hooks, beads, thread—you know—stuff for tying trout flies."

"You're going to make trout flies?" That was great news! It meant Dad knew he'd be fishing again—someday.

"I'm sick of crossword puzzles."

"Yeah," said Ellis. Dad's life was pretty boring. It didn't used to be. Ellis couldn't remember the last time they'd hiked or camped out. Or when Dad had gone canoeing or to a movie with Mom. Ellis wanted to blurt out, "Me and Tink—we're going to get you your life back," but what if his plan didn't work? He didn't want Dad to get his hopes up.

"What do woolly worms eat?" asked Ellis.

"Don't know," said Dad. "Grass?"

"What about Cheerios?"

Dad thought a minute, then said, "I doubt it."

Uh-oh, thought Ellis.

Dad pulled a pack of gum out of his shirt pocket. "Want one?"

"Sure."

They bounced along the curvy road that snaked to the Mast General Store, chewing gum. The juicy sweet smell filled up the Jeep.

If any place was likely to sell snacks for caterpillars or at least know what they ate, it was the Mast General Store. It was a Stone Age sort of place that carried odd stuff like Dr. LeGear's Cow Prescription and Barker's Lice Powder. Plus, older people hung out there who knew something about everything.

Ellis sprinted into the store so fast, he plowed straight into Mr. Mason.

"Whoa," said Mr. Mason, laughing and putting his hands on Ellis's shoulders.

"Sorry," said Ellis.

Ellis liked Mr. Mason. He collected fishing bobbers—the red-and-white round plastic floats that go on fishing line. Every Fourth of July he covered up his four-wheeler with them and drove in the parade. Ellis thought that showed way more imagination than collecting rocks or something.

Mr. Mason grinned at Dad and said, "Switched out that engine yet?" He was always trying to talk Dad into putting a V-8 engine in his Jeep.

Dad shook his head and said, "I like what I got."

"But Frank, I'm telling you—"

Ellis slipped away. He wandered past the post office section, with its small metal cubicles that had glass fronts and combination locks.

Ellis thought the whole place smelled like the inside of a covered wagon. Not that he'd ever been in a covered wagon, but he guessed it would smell like this. Old wood, metal parts, dried beans, beef jerky, and fresh air blowing through the open doors.

He looked for somebody to ask about woolly worm food. All the clerks were busy.

Next to the potbellied stove in the middle of the store, Mr. Beamer sat in a rocking chair playing checkers with Doc Swenson—two worn and wrinkly men with wads of chewing tobacco puffing out their cheeks.

They both nodded in Ellis's direction. He nodded back.

Doc used to be a veterinarian. Maybe he'd know what woolly worms ate.

Ellis walked over and said, "Excuse me."

Doc and Mr. Beamer both looked up from underneath white eyebrows as bushy as Tink. Doc leaned in close and squinted at Ellis. "Aren't you Frank and Mary Coffey's boy?"

"Yes, sir."

He reared back as if he'd discovered gold. "You've grown a foot."

"Yes, sir. Do you know what woolly worms eat?"

Mr. Beamer leaned forward to slide a root beer bottle cap onto the next square. Ellis didn't know if the board ever had real checkers, but everybody who played here had used bottle caps for as long as he could remember.

"Woolly worms are real partial to violets," Mr. Beamer drawled, as if Ellis had asked a perfectly normal question. "And lamb's-quarter. You know what lamb's-quarter is?"

"No sir," said Ellis. But what he was thinking was, Tink's going to starve.

Doc took an RC cola cap and jumped Mr. Beamer's A&W root beer cap, capturing it. Then he made a *humph* sound at Mr. Beamer. "Hogwash," he said with a sneer. "Why don't you tell him he has to find caviar and crumpets?" He spit out the *caviar and crumpets* part. Then he leaned back in his chair and said, "Listen to me, boy. Grass, green leaves, a little cabbage—that worm'll think he's gone to heaven."

Great, thought Ellis. He could find plenty of that. Now all he had to do was get home—fast. Tink needed food. How long could she go without eating?

Mr. Beamer shrugged. "You fellas suit yourself. Violets, grass. Don't matter. Just be ready for the frass."

"What's frass?" asked Ellis.

Mr. Beamer spit a wad of black gunk into a jar. Then he winked at Ellis and said, "You'll see."

Doc chuckled.

"Thanks," said Ellis. Who cared what frass was? Finally, he knew what to feed Tink.

He hurried through the store, looking for Dad. He slowed down as he passed the candy barrels. What would he buy if he had money? A Tootsie Pop? Gummy bears?

That's when Ellis spotted Alice. She was talking to her dad and wearing an orange baseball cap with her ponytail pulled through the back.

"It's your birthday," said her dad. "Pick out any candy you want."

Alice! thought Ellis. And it's her birthday.

Ellis had been so busy thinking about Dad and the thousand dollars, he'd almost forgotten that his woolly worm plan included Alice. If he won, he was going to give her Tink. But he wished he could give her something right now—for her birthday.

He looked around for free samples of something. Anything. Well, not *anything*. Red Man chewing tobacco would be crazy. So would a corncob pipe or a bag of nails. But it didn't matter, because there was nothing free, anyway.

"Hi, Alice," he muttered.

Alice smiled.

"Do you like animals?"

"Sure," said Alice. "I've got a golden retriever and two hamsters. What about you?"

"Uh, no. Well, I sort of have a cat, but not really."

Alice seemed to be waiting for an explanation.

"I mean, do you like to read about different animals? You know—like moose and anteaters and lemurs."

"Yeah," said Alice, looking interested. "Lemurs live in Madagascar."

"Yeah, they eat fruit and leaves," said Ellis.

"Except for the ones that eat only bamboo," Alice added.

"Right!" Ellis was impressed. "Uh, do you like woolly worms?"

"Um, sure," said Alice. "Do you have one?" She stared at his hands to see if he was holding one.

"Yes, I mean, no. I mean, I found one, but it's at home."

"You should race it at the Woolly Worm Festival," said Alice.

"Yeah," said Ellis. "I will."

"Good luck," said Alice.

Silence filled the space between them.

Now what? thought Ellis. He tried to think of something funny. "Did you know that I can burp 'The Star-Spangled Banner'?" he bragged.

"What? Uh, no," said Alice, turning back to the candy barrels.

"Do you want to hear it?"

"No thanks."

Maybe she'd like something funnier, thought Ellis. He clamped his hand under his armpit and tried to make a disgusting sound, but all that came out was a wimpy clap.

Alice ignored him. Maybe she didn't have a sense of humor.

Ellis spotted a wastebasket full of bubble-gum and candy wrappers that customers had thrown away. They were all different colors. Close by, a fan sat on the floor, its blades whirling on high speed.

Ellis grabbed a handful of wrappers and tossed them into the fan. Instant flying confetti!

Bright flecks of paper spun up and over Alice. Orange, red, purple, green, and blue. She laughed and tried to grab some, but they all swirled out of her reach.

"Happy birthday," he said.

"Thanks," said Alice, still smiling at all the tiny colors drifting to the floor.

"Alice," called her dad. "It's time."

"I've got to go," said Alice. Quickly, she filled her basket with a dozen different pieces of candy. "See you at school." She grinned, then waved good-bye.

Ellis bent over and began to pick up all the candy-wrapper confetti. He was pretty sure he'd finally done something right.

8 MAGIC CATERPILLAR MUD

"What's frass?" Ellis asked his dad on the ride home.

"Never heard of it," answered Dad.

Ellis decided it couldn't be all that important. *Grass* was what was important—it was caterpillar food. He couldn't wait to feed some to Tink.

But when the Jeep pulled up to their house, the first thing Ellis noticed was the porch ferns. If plants could wheeze, those ferns were gasping for breath.

He'd forgotten to water them.

Tink first, Ellis decided. Feeding her would be quick. Then he'd water the ferns. Meanwhile, Dad was pretending to walk like normal into the house, but he couldn't disguise a small limp, which meant his pain pills had worn off.

Ellis got him his medicine and a glass of water. Then he

ran upstairs to check on Tink. He flung the lid off the shoe box. She was alive!

She wasn't exactly zipping around, but her eyes were open. Ellis thought they had a frantic searching look—kind of like his did when he rummaged through the refrigerator looking for a snack after school.

"One feast, coming up," said Ellis. He hurried back downstairs, ran outside, pulled up a handful of grass, picked a fresh green leaf, and sprinted back to his room.

He stacked the tiny mound of grass clippings in one corner of her box and placed the green leaf in the other. "Chow time!" he announced.

Tink didn't dash over to eat, but she did do her bobble-head hiccup nod.

Ellis nodded back. He watched her. "Come on, Tink," he whispered. "You've got to eat." He pushed the green leaf across the box until it was right next to her face. Nothing.

Ellis whispered, "This is the most delicious leaf on the planet. Woolly worms all over the world would kill for this leaf. You are soooo lucky."

Still nothing.

Maybe she needed privacy again.

Ellis replaced the lid. Silently, he counted to a hundred, then lifted the lid for a peek.

Tink hunched her body and sent Ellis a feeling that clearly said, *Go away.*

Ellis closed the lid. He smiled. Tink had attitude. That meant she wasn't dying.

Ellis went back downstairs and started soaking the ferns in the sink. While each one soaked, Ellis looked up *frass* in the dictionary. He flipped pages until he found the word *Fraser*—a river in Canada. The next word was *fraternal*—meaning "brotherly." *Frass* should've been between them.

Ellis's parents' dictionary wasn't very big. Maybe *frass* would be in Mr. Turnmire's. He'd have to wait and look it up at school on Monday.

What had Mr. Beamer said? Be ready for frass? Or *beware* of frass?

Ellis soaked another fern, then cleaned up all the equipment they'd used this summer to sell blueberries. First he rinsed the plastic gallon milk jugs—the ones they'd cut the tops off of and run strings through. That way anyone who wanted to pick his own could hang a container around his neck, drop the berries in, and still have both hands free to pick.

Ellis switched out the fern in the sink and hoped Tink was upstairs eating.

He tested all the garden hoses for leaks, then unscrewed them so they wouldn't freeze and burst their pipes over the winter. Ellis circled them into neat loops.

He soaked another fern and hoped he could find string to make Tink's racetrack.

He stacked their cardboard flats—the boxes they used to spread the berries out to dry in so they wouldn't get smushed. Then he counted how many cases of canning jars Mom had left over after making a gazillion batches of jam.

The whole time, Ellis practiced his whispering. "On your mark, get set, go, Tink! Run. Race. Go for the gold! You can do it, you can do it, you can, you can!"

Ellis wondered which was more important—*what* he said or *how* he said it?

He watered another fern, then arranged everything in the storage shed—all of it counted, cleaned up, and ready to go for next year.

He soaked the last fern and went back to Tink. He opened the lid of her box. Half the leaf was nibbled away and most of the grass was gone! Ellis pumped his fist and shouted, "Yes!"

What was all that other stuff?

The bottom of the box was covered with tiny chunks of

something that looked like dark green hairballs—without the hair. Had Tink thrown up?

"Are you okay?" asked Ellis.

Tink turned the head end of her body toward Ellis and smiled. Well . . . not a smile exactly because he couldn't see her mouth—just fuzz. But she looked happy. Her head was cocked in a way that seemed to say, "I'm good. Thanks for asking."

He sniffed the small, dark blobs. They smelled kind of earthy. Whatever they were, they were making a mess.

"Hey, Tink," Ellis whispered. "If you crawl onto my palm, I'll clean up your castle." He lowered his hand into the box. "Do you copy?"

Tink wiggled her face in front of his hand as if she were smelling him, then climbed on.

"Roger," whispered Ellis. "Over and out."

Her feet tickled.

He carried her box outside with his other hand and dumped everything out. He put the rocks and spongy stick back in with new twigs and leaves and grass. Tink wiggled on his shoulder and watched.

"Now, *I* have to eat lunch," he explained, lowering her into the box. "You get some rest because after lunch I'm going to train you to race."

Tink crawled under the spongy stick and curled up. Then she bobbed her head a fraction as if to say, "Ten-four, over and out."

Ellis found Dad in the living room, lying down with his trout-fly supplies spread out around him. He gripped a tiny hook that he'd already transformed into some kind of bug. He held it close to his nose, squinting to see well enough to wrap thread around it.

Ellis headed into the kitchen. Mom had thawed some vegetable soup, so Ellis heated it, spooned it into two bowls, and took one to Dad.

"Look." Dad held up his finished trout fly. It looked kind of like a wasp with a tiny gold bead for a head. "Isn't it a beauty?"

"Yeah. It is. What's it called?"

"An Evil Weevil Nymph."

"If I were a trout, I'd be all over it," said Ellis.

Dad smiled with satisfaction.

Ellis sat across from him and shoveled soup into his mouth. The first spoonful burned his tongue.

"You're slurping," said Dad.

"I'm starving."

Dad nodded, blew on his soup, and took a small sip. "You're going to burn your tongue.

"Already did," said Ellis.

"Slow down," said Dad, but Ellis knew he was proud that Ellis hadn't whined about it.

"Can't," said Ellis. "Too hungry." Plus, he was in a hurry to get back to Tink.

He polished off his soup, then took his empty bowl to the kitchen. He popped two ice cubes in his mouth to soothe his tongue and raced back upstairs.

Oh man, the little blobs were back. What *was* that stuff? Magic caterpillar mud? Vomit?

Was it poop? Ellis sniffed it again. Same smell as before—earthy but not stinky like poop. Besides, there was way too much of it.

Even I don't poop *that* much, thought Ellis.

He lifted Tink out and tried to say, "Walk across my

hand." But it came out, "Wah ahcra ma ham" because he still had a mouthful of ice.

He crunched up the ice, swallowed it, and tried again: "Walk across my hand." He made sure he sounded firm, but nice.

Tink did it—she walked across his hand.

"Climb my arm," he whispered.

She climbed straight up his arm, all the way to his shoulder.

Ellis couldn't believe it!

"Circle my neck three times!" he cried.

Tink turned and wiggled back off in the direction of his elbow.

Maybe he'd gotten too excited. Had he jerked his arm? Was he too loud? Or did she just not *want* to circle his neck?

He tried to remember how his voice had sounded when she'd done what he said. He wasn't sure. This worm-whispering thing was going to be harder than he'd thought.

Ellis sprawled across his bed and decided to let Tink do whatever she wanted.

"Look around," he urged. "Have fun."

Tink wriggled under his pillow.

"You're a great woolly worm," he called after her. "A wiggly winner. A world-class wonder."

She backed her butt out a tiny fraction of an inch and wiggled it.

Ellis grinned. "That's right," he said. "Enjoy yourself. Relax. We've got all the time in the world."

Except, they didn't.

9 ALL GOD'S CREATURES

Sunday morning, Ellis rolled over in bed. He opened his eyes and stretched his arms up toward the ceiling. Then he leaped out of bed to look at Tink.

She was curled in one corner because there wasn't enough space in the box for her to move. The bottom of the box was littered with more of the hairball things.

"Ellis!" called Mom. "Time for church."

"Coming," he answered. Church—at least the part with the sermon—was more boring than a pile of dead ants. But he liked Sunday school because he got to be with other kids.

Ellis cleaned Tink's box. Then he pulled on his white Sunday shirt and navy blue pants and went downstairs to breakfast—frozen blueberries and Cheerios.

Mom handed him the bowl and smiled. She wore a

green print dress that made her look nice—except for the dark circles under her eyes.

"There's blueberry bread, too," she offered.

Ellis wanted to say, *Wow, blueberries, yum*—just to be funny. But Mom thought sarcasm was one of the seven deadly sins.

"Thanks," he answered, slicing off a chunk of blueberry bread. Then he tore off a square of paper towel and put the bread on it.

"Don't waste paper towels," said Mom, sitting down and sipping her coffee. "Use a plate."

"Okay." But, he'd already used the paper towel. It had crumbs on it, and a squished-blueberry stain. If he got a plate now, it wouldn't change the fact that the paper towel was already used.

He wondered what would make Mom happier—keeping the paper towel or throwing the paper towel away. He pulled a plate out of the cabinet and slid his bread onto it. The paper towel would be his napkin.

"Where's the butter?" Ellis didn't see it anywhere—no familiar tub of homemade creamy yellow butter sitting on the counter.

Mom reached back and swung open the refrigerator door. She pulled out a stick of store-bought margarine.

"I don't have time to make butter anymore," said Mom. She stated it like a science fact—water freezes at thirty-two degrees; the human heart beats a hundred thousand times a day.

Ellis stared. His mother loved homemade butter. If there were an eighth deadly sin, margarine would be it. What else had she given up that he didn't know about?

He sliced off a pat of margarine and tried to spread it on his bread. It wasn't soft like Mom's homemade butter, so it ripped a hole in the bread. Ellis wadded it all up before his mom could see what the evil margarine had done and popped it into his mouth. "Mmm," he said. "Good."

Mom nodded absentmindedly and brushed her hair wisps back with one wrist. "Don't forget your Bible," said Mom.

"Oh yeah." Ellis went back up to his room. He lifted the lid of Tink's box one last time.

Tink munched on a leaf.

Ellis hated to leave her. "Want to go to church?" he joked.

Tink tilted her head.

Ellis felt her curiosity. He didn't know if Tink would like church or not. But having her to play with while the preacher talked way too long about stuff Ellis already knew seemed like a great idea.

"Church," Ellis repeated. "You get to ride in a truck. Want to come?"

Tink's head did her hiccup move.

"Great," said Ellis. Frantically, he scanned his room for something safe to carry her in. Something big enough that she wouldn't get squashed but small enough to hide from his mother. Mom believed that taking insects to church was another deadly sin. He knew because of the time he'd taken a june bug.

"Ellis!" called Mom.

"Coming." He grabbed his Bible and looked one last time for something to put Tink in. He gave up and eased her into his shirt's front pocket.

Ellis sat cross-legged on the dark green area rug on the floor of his Sunday school class. Nine other students sat with him, forming a half circle around their teacher, Miss Bluford.

Alice, Molly, Randy, and George sat close to Ellis in the circle.

Ellis liked Miss Bluford. She was a short, round lady who liked to laugh and clap her hands with joy. She opened her arms wide and said, "Let the little children come to me, and do not hinder them, for the kingdom of heaven belongs to such as these."

Ellis felt Tink on the move. She had stayed in his pocket, all curled up, for the whole ride to church with Mom, but now she was inching her way out.

"Stay," hissed Ellis at his pocket. Tink froze just out of sight.

"Who said that?" asked Miss Bluford.

"I did," said Ellis. "Sorry."

The class laughed. Randy, who was sitting next to Ellis, elbowed him and said, "You idiot. Jesus said that—not you."

"Jesus said, *Stay*?" asked Ellis, confused.

"Ellis," explained Miss Bluford. "I was asking the class, who said, 'Let the little children come to me'? Randy is correct. Jesus did say that. Who can tell me why he said it?"

"Because"—Molly raised her hand, but didn't wait to be called on—"his disciples were yelling at the parents for bringing their children straight up to Jesus. They said Jesus had better things to do than mess with a bunch of dumb kids."

"Well," said Miss Bluford, "that's not exactly how His disciples said it, but you have the right idea. Who can tell me some of the things Jesus taught them?"

"Blessed are the meek, because they will inherit the earth," said Alice.

"Forgive people," said George.

"Do unto others," said Billy.

"Get back in there!" cried Ellis. Tink's head was peeking out above Ellis's shirt pocket.

"Eeeek!" exclaimed Molly. "What *is* that?"

"Awesome," said George. "Ellis has hair on his chest."

"It's not hair," Randy scoffed. "It moves."

"What do you have in your pocket?" asked Miss Bluford.

Ellis was so busted. He'd wanted to keep Tink hidden.

But there she was—all thirteen fuzzy bands of her creeping out of his pocket and up onto his collar.

"One of God's creatures," answered Ellis.

"Quick thinking," whispered George.

"Give me it," said Randy, snatching Tink off Ellis's collar and dangling her in the air.

"Stop!" cried Alice.

Ellis lunged at Randy. "Don't!"

"Children!" said Miss Bluford, clapping her hands but not for joy. "That's enough. Randy, give Ellis back his caterpillar."

"It's a woolly worm," said Alice.

"I can see that," said Miss Bluford.

Reluctantly, Randy handed Tink back to Ellis.

"You okay?" asked Ellis.

Tink looked up at him, dazed but unhurt.

"Ellis," said Miss Bluford. "Would you like to tell us about your woolly worm?"

"No. I mean, yes. I mean yes, ma'am," said Ellis. He didn't want to tell them anything. Not yet. But they were all looking at him expectantly. Like he was important.

He cleared his throat. "She does what I tell her." Ellis sucked in a giant breath of air and hoped that that was true. "Watch this." He placed Tink in his cupped hand, jiggled her a little, and said, "Play dead."

Tink curled into a ball.

"Anybody can do that," said Randy.

"Oh yeah?" said Ellis. "How about this?" He placed Tink on the back of his hand and whispered, "Walk across my hand."

Tink stretched out her body and gripped his knuckles with her tiny feet, but she didn't move.

"Walk across my hand," he repeated, softer. "Please. You know—like you did at home."

Tink crawled across his hand.

"Wonderful!" Miss Bluford clapped her hands—this time with joy.

The class cheered.

"Go, woolly worm," said George.

Ellis moved Tink from his hand to the middle of his outstretched arm. "Crawl up my arm," he whispered.

Tink began to inch her way down toward his open palm.

"That's *down* your arm," said Randy, "Not up."

"So?" said George. "It's still crawling . . . on his arm . . . like he said."

Had Ellis's voice been too phony? Too loud? Should he have said *please*?

Ellis plucked Tink off his wrist. "We're still working out the details," he mumbled. He placed Tink on the floor and everyone watched her inch her way across the green carpet. "We're entering the Woolly Worm Race next Saturday."

He hadn't meant to say that. It just came out.

"Excellent," said Miss Bluford, clapping joyfully again. "Now, let's all join hands and sing. I think we all know the perfect hymn for Ellis's caterpillar."

Randy gagged.

Molly turned to Randy and whispered, "You will *not* inherit the earth."

Then they all sang,

All things bright and beautiful,
All creatures great and small,
All things wise and wonderful,
The Lord God made them all.

Tink raised her body up and bent it as if she was taking a bow. Ellis felt her happiness swell in his own chest.

After Sunday school, everyone clustered around Ellis in the hall. They all wanted to hold Tink.

This is a lot easier than trying to be funny, thought

Ellis. "From now on," he whispered to Tink, "you go every-where with me."

As they passed her around, Ellis reached to get her back before Randy got a turn.

Too late.

Randy had her, and he'd bolted for the door.

Ellis pushed his way through the hallway that was filling up with kids getting out of other classes. He flung open the door and ran after Randy.

By the time he caught up, Randy stood in the grass in front of the church, palms up, empty-handed. "All God's creatures should be free," he said.

10 RESCUE

"Where is she?" Ellis shouted at Randy.

"She?" laughed Randy. "Your woolly worm's a girl? How do you even know that? Does she have—?"

"Give her back!" yelled Ellis.

"Can't," Randy shrugged. "I set it free. I mean, her. I set *her* free."

"Where?" cried Ellis, looking down, suddenly afraid he might be standing on Tink.

Randy shrugged again.

Ellis balled his hands up into two fists. "Show me," he said through clenched teeth. "Show me where you put her or I'll—"

"Or you'll what?" Randy interrupted. "Crack lame jokes until I die laughing?" He turned to go.

"I mean it," said Ellis. He shoved Randy's shoulder.

Randy turned to face him. Ellis drew back one arm. He'd never hit anybody in the face before.

"You're going to beat me up?" Randy grinned and backed up a step. "I hope you brought help."

"He did," said George.

Ellis whirled around and saw George marching toward them. He had the same don't-mess-with-me expression that Dad had when he'd saved Ellis from the rattlesnake.

"Tell him where you hid the caterpillar," said George. "Or you'll be sorry."

"Go ahead," said Randy. "Hit me. Tackle me. We can all roll around kicking and punching and squashing whatever's crawling on the ground."

"Wait," said Ellis, "don't anybody move." He dropped to his knees and began separating blades of grass.

"Here?" asked George. "His woolly worm's right here?"

"Maybe." Randy shrugged. "Maybe not."

George clenched his fists and made a move toward Randy.

"No," said Ellis. "Don't hit him. He might fall on her."

"Give me a break," said Randy. "You couldn't knock me over if you had a bulldozer.

George opened his hands back up and rubbed them as though he was massaging them. "Randy," he said calmly, "tell us where you put the caterpillar, or you *will* be sorry."

Ellis stared at George. So did Randy.

The firmness in his voice didn't sound like George. It sounded like Rambo.

"You guys are crazy," said Randy. "It's just a stupid bug. Maybe it's over by those rocks." Randy pointed.

Ellis stood up and tip-toed toward the four large stones where Randy was pointing. They had pink flowers planted around them. All the way there he watched where he put his feet. George followed him, just as carefully.

"What a jerk," said Ellis, squatting by one of the rocks and looking underneath the flowers.

"Yeah," said George. He knelt across from Ellis and

carefully began to explore the rock crevices with his fingers.

"What's wrong with him?" asked Ellis.

"Who knows?" said George. "Mom says he does it for attention."

"*Bad* attention?" asked Ellis.

George shrugged, "Doesn't make sense to me, either."

"I've got to find Tink," said Ellis, prying up the corner of one of the rocks. "What if she's not here?"

"She?" asked George. "Your caterpillar? It's a girl?"

"Yep," said Ellis.

George laughed, "You're so funny."

"Thanks," Ellis forced a grin. He hadn't meant to be funny. He should tell George more about Tink. And worm whispering. And Dad.

Instead he called, "Wooooo," in a spooky voice. "You are in my power. Cooome to me."

George laughed.

Ellis grinned.

"If we don't find her, I'll help you look for another one," said George.

"Great," Ellis answered, trying to sound grateful. But inside, his heart felt heavier than the rock he was lifting up. He didn't want another woolly worm. He wanted

Tink. He wasn't sure he could communicate with another caterpillar the way he could with her.

"You okay?" asked George.

"Sure," Ellis lied. When it came to serious stuff, he wondered why it was easier to talk to ducks than to people.

"Hey!" exclaimed George. He reached down and pulled a small furry creature from one of the crevices. "I found her!"

Ellis looked at the pattern of bands. Two dark, nine light, two dark—a cold start and a cold end, with a little over two mild months in the middle. "It's her!" cried Ellis.

George put Tink onto Ellis's open palm. She raised her body into the air and swiveled it with attitude.

Ellis stroked her fuzzy head with one finger and said, "Thanks, George."

"No problem," he answered. "But I've got to go, or I'm going to be late for church." He waved and took off running.

Church, thought Ellis.

He raised Tink up to nose level and spoke to her in the firmest voice he could manage. "You are about to enter the House of God. I'm going to put you in my pocket, and when I say 'Stay,' I mean it."

When Ellis walked into church beside his mother. Tink was curled up tight inside his shirt pocket.

Ellis spotted friendly Mrs. Paisley walking up the aisle, hugging every person she met along the way.

"Ellis," she said, spreading her arms in welcome. "My, but you have grown!"

Ellis eyed her with dread. She was as big as a mountain, wore dresses shaped like circus tents, and loved to hug. If she got her arms around him, she'd squeeze the life out of Tink.

Ellis shivered. The image was so real he thought he could actually hear the squishy noise Tink would make as she became a caterpillar pancake, her insides oozing out like blackberry jam.

He slid into the nearest pew, tugging his mother along with him.

"Ellis?" asked Mom. What—?"

"I like this row," said Ellis.

Mom sat down, shaking her head.

Ellis slumped against the back of the pew. "Don't worry," he whispered into his shirt pocket, "I won't let Mrs. Paisley anywhere near you."

"Who are you talking to?" asked Mom.

"Nobody."

Ellis settled in. He looked for George or Alice, but all he saw were big, grown-up bodies all around him. A sixth-grade girl at the end of his row had a book in her lap that wasn't the Bible. Ellis wished he had his library book.

Everyone stood to sing the opening hymn. The organ pipes filled the church with the music to "Faith of Our Fathers." Ellis felt Tink stir in his pocket. "Be still," he whispered.

As voices surged around him, Tink tapped all her feet in his pocket.

Mom held the hymnal out for Ellis to share. Ellis held his half with his left hand. He placed his right hand over the top of his pocket. Tink pushed her head against his pinky. She felt like a tiny scrub brush scraping against his finger. Was she dancing?

"Be still," Ellis hissed into his pocket. Tink's feet moved faster.

"You're a good worm," Ellis whispered more kindly as Mom and the congregation sang. "Please calm down," he added.

Tink grew quiet when the music stopped.

Ellis sank back in his seat and listened to the scripture lesson and the sermon. He doodled on one of the collection envelopes in the wooden rack on the back of the pew in front of him. With the stubby pencil, he drew a picture of Tink. He put tiny track shoes on all of her feet. Ellis wanted to take her out and let her crawl on his hand where Mom couldn't see, but she hadn't moved in his pocket since the opening hymn. Ellis guessed she was asleep. Pastor Parks's voice was making him sleepy too.

Ellis wanted to be home, training Tink. The race was six days away, and he hadn't even built her a racetrack yet.

The sermon seemed to last a week. Finally, Pastor Parks wrapped up with a really long prayer. Then the organist played the first notes of the closing hymn. Tink stirred in Ellis's pocket.

Members of the congregation flipped noisily through the pages of their hymnals and stood up. Ellis heard Mrs. Paisley's knees pop three pews up. The tall man sitting on the other side of him coughed into his handkerchief, then stood.

Voices filled the church. Deep voices, high-pitched voices, all came together and swelled like a rising wave.

Tink's feet were on the move again.

"No," said Ellis.

His words were drowned out by the congregation, which was singing, *"Onward, Christian soldiers, marching as to war."*

Tink's feet marched, too—straight out of Ellis's pocket and onto his neck.

Ellis plucked her off and dropped her back into his pocket.

"Stay!" he hissed.

Mom shot him a look.

"Forward into battle, see His banners go," sang the congregation.

Tink marched out of his pocket again. He grabbed for her and missed. Tink toppled to the floor, curled up into a ball, and rolled under Ellis's seat.

He dropped down, trying to find her. He groped under the pew, feeling nothing but bare floor.

And then he saw her. She was marching again, onto the shoe of the man next to Ellis, over his pants cuff, and up his leg.

The man didn't spot Tink, but he definitely noticed Ellis, crouched on the floor. He frowned down at him.

Ellis didn't know what to do. He couldn't just snatch Tink off the man's pants.

To Ellis's relief, the man turned his attention back to his hymnal and continued to sing.

Ellis watched as Tink climbed the man's leg, circled behind his knee, then dropped onto the long bench. Still marching, she advanced across the pew, heading for Mom's seat.

Mom stooped toward Ellis. "Stand up," she said, holding out his half of the hymnal again.

"Don't sit!" cried Ellis.

Ellis stood up and scrambled past his mother just as Tink reached the end of the pew. He grabbed Tink. Then he whispered to his mother, "Gotta go—bathroom."

The voices rose around him, singing, *"Satan's host doth flee,"* as Ellis dashed up the aisle.

Ellis rushed out of the sanctuary and into cool mountain air. He waited for his mother in the truck.

"Are you okay?" she asked, opening the door and sliding behind the driver's seat.

"Yep."

"What was all that about?"

"What?"

"Talking to your pocket, running out of church, acting like—"

"Let's listen to the radio," said Ellis, reaching forward and twisting the knob.

"Fine," said Mom, "but—"

"Knock, knock," said Ellis.

Mom wrinkled up her face at him, then sighed and answered, "Who's there?"

"Radio."

"Radio, who?"

"Radio not, here I come."

Mom laughed. Then she punched the setting for her favorite radio station and hummed along to "What a Friend We Have in Jesus." The wrinkly lines on her face smoothed out.

Ellis felt Tink's feet moving to the beat. No, he thought. Not again. Not now. He jiggled his pocket until she curled back into a ball.

I've got a marching, dancing caterpillar, thought Ellis. But I need one that can race.

11 CHORES, CHILD LABOR, TRAINING

"Don't forget your chores," said Mom as she pulled up to the house.

Chores! thought Ellis.

But he answered, "Yes, ma'am."

Then Mom turned the truck around and headed back to church to do something she'd volunteered for. Ellis shook his head and watched her disappear down their driveway. Sunday was the only day off she had.

Ellis placed Tink in her box and promised to be back soon. Then he put in a load of laundry, emptied the trash, and dusted the living room.

Dad was stretched out flat in his recliner. Materials for tying flies were spread out around him, along with tools to fix a lamp Mom had dug out of a dumpster. Apparently, he'd abandoned both projects, because he was working on a crossword puzzle. "What's a seven-letter word for *against the law*? It has two *l*'s in it."

Ellis waved his feather duster in the air, and said, "Child labor." He knew it was two words and too many letters, but that answer was so hilarious he couldn't stop himself.

"Very funny," grumbled Dad. But he grinned.

Ellis swooped the duster up and down the window blinds, making a rippling clacking noise. Next, he swept the porch. *Swoof.* He swung the broom across a big stick. *Swish.* He whooshed the broom across some leaves.

Done. Finally. *Now* he could train Tink.

Meow.

Ellis looked down and saw Ginger circling his legs. Up close, she looked terrible—super skinny with burrs stuck in her fur.

Ellis tip-toed into the kitchen and poured milk into a bowl and carried it upstairs to his room. "I'm back!" he called to Tink. "I didn't forget you."

Ellis slid his window open and placed the milk on the sill. Ginger knew how to reach it by climbing onto the porch roof under his window.

As soon as he put the milk down, she was there, lapping it up in greedy gulps and getting a milk mustache.

Ellis knew he wasn't supposed to feed her, but she looked awful—he couldn't let her starve.

Ginger licked the bowl clean. "You have to go." Ellis gently pushed Ginger out so he could close the window. She rubbed up against the glass once, twice, and then she was gone.

Ellis lifted the lid on Tink's box. More mess. Geez. He decided to ignore it. He was ready to race.

"Tink, do you copy?"

She lifted the top half of her body up, swiveling it to face him.

Okay, thought Ellis. She hears me, but does she understand me?

"Ready to race?"

Tink stretched her body straight up, as if she wanted Ellis to lift her out of the box.

Ellis picked her up and asked her to crawl across his hand.

She did.

Encouraged, he said, "Crawl up my arm."

She stopped, lifted her head, and gazed at him as if to say, make up your mind.

He tapped his elbow to show her the direction in which he wanted her to move.

She didn't budge—not a hair. She seemed to be waiting. Waiting for what? Ellis wondered.

"Onward, Christian soldiers," he sang softly.

He thought he saw her head sway, slightly.

A bit louder, he continued, *"marching as to war."* He tapped the crook of his elbow again to show her where he wanted her to go as he continued to sing.

Tink's tiny feet began to march up the inside of his arm, tickling as they went.

"Yes!" shouted Ellis.

Tink stopped and curled herself into a ball so fast that she rolled off his arm, hit the floor, and rolled under his bed.

Ellis dropped to his hands and knees. "I'm sorry. Tink. Hey! I'm so sorry. You okay? Where are you?" He blew away several dust balls and scooped her up into his hands.

"My fault," he apologized into the cup of his hand. "You were doing great!" he cheered. When Tink remained curled, he remembered Mrs. Puckett and the horse, and repeated, more soothingly, "You did great." Then he sang softly, *"This little light of mine, I'm gonna let it shine."*

Her body began to uncurl. Then she stretched just like a dog waking up from a nap, with the lower third of her body bent up in the air.

Ellis placed her on his bed and watched her flatten out

and explore the little valleys where his quilt was stitched. Finally, he asked, "Are you ready to race?"

Tink lifted her head, stared at Ellis, and did her hiccup head bounce.

Ellis almost cheered, but he didn't. Instead he said quietly, "Perfect. Wait here."

Ellis ran a string from the bottom of his windowsill to the top and kept it in place with duct tape. He placed Tink on the bottom of the string and said, "Go."

She looked at him.

Maybe he'd said it too loudly. He leaned in close and whispered, "Go."

She still didn't move. Flashbacks of Chester played through his head.

"Onward, Christian soldiers," he sang.

Thump! Ginger hit the windowpane. *Blap! Blap!* She was up on her hind legs, batting at the glass. Trying to get to Tink.

Ellis snatched Tink off the string.

She coiled up into a tight ball in Ellis's hand.

"Tink, it's okay," said Ellis in his calmest voice. "It was a cat. But she's gone. I won't let her hurt you." Ellis stroked her back. "Tink, I promise, it's okay. Talk to me."

Tink stayed curled up in his hand. If she had a thumb, she'd be sucking it. He tried humming a few bars of "What a Friend We Have in Jesus."

Nothing.

He didn't know if she was still playing dead because the cat had scared her or because he stunk as a worm whisperer.

Reluctantly, Ellis placed Tink back in her box and closed the lid.

Now what? Tink was too traumatized to train. Tomorrow he had school all day.

He wouldn't get to train Tink until the afternoon, but at least he'd get to borrow Mr. Turnmire's dictionary and find out what frass was.

12 FRASS IS FREAKY

Monday morning, Ellis woke up early.

"Tink," he called, "how'd you sleep? You still scared?"

Ellis lifted the lid on her box. Tink wasn't there. He lifted one of the rocks and spotted her.

She flinched and shrank up as if she'd been caught with no clothes on. Then she crawled under a leaf.

"Sorry," said Ellis. "Look, today's going to be great. You'll see. Right now I'm going to clean your caterpillar castle." It was full of the blobs again.

What if he took some of it to school and passed it around as snack food? Munch on a lunch with extra crunch. *That* would be funny.

Ellis picked up all of Tink's blobs and dropped them into a Baggie. Then he placed fresh food in her box.

She raised herself as if she wanted to be picked up.

Ellis wished he could take her to school, but no way. He

hadn't forgotten church and Sunday school. Looking after her had proven downright dangerous.

"You're safer here," he said. "And I'll be back this afternoon. Then you can show me how fast you are."

Tink swiveled her head in every direction. Ellis got a jittery feeling in his chest—Tink was nervous.

"No cat," he promised.

Tink bobbed her head.

Ellis stroked her back, hummed two bars of "This Little Light of Mine," and then he gently closed the lid.

As soon as Ellis got to school, he bolted for Mr. Turnmire's giant dictionary. He flipped through the *f*'s, looking for *frass*. And there it was:

frass: insect refuse. Excrement left behind by an insect or insect larvae.

The only word he understood was *insect*. So he looked up *refuse*, and discovered that it meant "garbage." Insect garbage? Tink had garbage?

He didn't understand. So he looked up *excrement*.

excrement: the body's solid waste matter, composed of undigested food and bacteria.

It *was* poop!

This, thought Ellis, is the best show-and-tell ever.

Ellis slid into his seat and slipped the Baggie into his desk drawer. Mr. Turnmire was writing the day's vocabulary word on the board:

humanitarian

"Who can tell me what that means?" Mr. Turnmire underlined the word.

"Mr. Turnmire!" Ellis waved his hand energetically. "Can we have show-and-tell now?"

"Not yet."

"My show-and-tell is the best vocabulary word you've ever heard!"

"*This* is the vocabulary word," said Mr. Turnmire, pointing again. "Can you tell me what it means?"

Ellis studied the word. He sounded it out slowly in his head. Hu - man - i - tar - ian. He tried it another way. Human - i - tarian. "I know!" he said.

Mr. Turnmire motioned for him to answer.

"It's a person who eats humans," said Ellis.

Mr. Turnmire stared, then shook his head. "No, Ellis. A cannibal eats humans. A humanitarian *helps* them."

"That doesn't make any sense," said Ellis.

Mr. Turnmire raised an eyebrow.

"If a vegetarian eats vegetables," said Ellis, squinting to make his face look serious, "then a humanitarian must eat humans."

The whole class laughed.

Ellis grinned.

Mr. Turnmire sighed and asked everyone to get out their books for free reading time.

Ellis opened up *All About Ants*. Alice sat across from him. She was reading a book in the same series, *All About Butterflies and Moths*.

Ellis held up his book and pointed at the title.

Alice smiled.

He tried to read, but he couldn't concentrate.

Finally, Mr. Turnmire said, "Time for show-and-tell."

Ellis waved his hand wildly. "Can I go first?"

He nodded.

Ellis pulled out his Baggie and rushed to the front of the room.

"This," he said, holding it high, "is frass."

"Looks like yuck," said Randy.

"What's frass?" asked George.

Mr. Turnmire squinted and looked closer.

"Frass," said Ellis, and then he hesitated. His presentation needed suspense.

"Can everyone please give me a drumroll?"

The class strummed their fingers on their desktops.

"Frass," Ellis repeated, holding it even higher, "is cater-pillar poop."

"Coooool," ooohed half the class.

"Grooooss," moaned the other half.

There were choruses of, "Pass it around!" and "I wanna touch it," and "I wanna flush it."

"Class," Mr. Turnmire raised one hand high. That meant *be quiet*. "Ellis has found something interesting. *And* he's taught us a new word."

"Exactly," said Ellis.

"You must've found a whole army of caterpillars," observed Mr. Turnmire.

"Nope," said Ellis. "Just one. It's freaky how much frass there is."

Everybody shouted stuff like, "Eeew," "No way," and "That's nasty."

"Her name's Tink."

"That's a dumb name," said Randy.

"No, it's not," said Ellis. "She likes it."

"Really?" said Randy. "Did she tell you?"

"Yeah," said Ellis. "As a matter of fact she did."

And then the whole class laughed out loud. Because they thought he was trying to be funny.

Ellis wanted to explain. He wanted to say he was a worm whisperer. That he wasn't trying to make them laugh—he was trying to win money for his dad's deductible. It wasn't funny. Not funny at all.

But they wouldn't understand.

"Thank you for sharing," said Mr. Turnmire.

Ellis slipped back into his seat and shoved the Baggie into his desk. Being funny was complicated.

He noticed Alice looking at him. She wasn't laughing. He was pretty sure she wasn't a fan of frass.

But, after class, Alice, Molly, and George walked up to him.

Alice said, "Ellis. You should bring Tink to school."

Was she joking? Had she forgotten the Sunday school disaster?

"Yeah," said Molly. "So we can see her again. And hear her talk."

"Yeah," said George. "Besides telling you her name, what else does she say?"

"Well . . ." Ellis hesitated. Okay. If they wanted funny, that's what he'd give them. "She likes music." Ellis marched in place and sang, *"Onward, Christian soldiers, marching as to war."*

George snorted.

Molly giggled.

Alice tilted her head.

Then Ellis burped "The Star-Spangled Banner."

George laughed out loud and suggested that they all belch "Row, Row, Row Your Boat" in rounds. Alice and Molly rolled their eyes at each other.

"Here," said Ellis, opening the Baggie full of frass. "Who wants a snack?" He reached in and pretended to chuck a few in his mouth.

George laughed so hard he double snorted. Molly gagged, and Alice rolled her eyes again.

Ellis thought he might be the funniest kid on the planet. But it didn't feel as good as it was supposed to.

He wished he hadn't let them turn Tink into a joke.

13   MISSING

When Ellis got home from school, he went straight to Tink. More frass.

"Man," he whispered. "If you race as well as you poop, we'll be rich."

He surveyed his room for a new place to stretch Tink's string—one that Ginger couldn't come anywhere near.

Ellis's room had a bed, a chest of drawers, a bedside table with a cubby for his books, and a small box for toys. Hanging on one wall he had a corkboard filled with his animal postcards from Gram and Pops. There was one window, but he couldn't use that because Ginger might attack it again. And there were two doors—one to the hall and one for his closet.

Ellis decided to use a door. He tied one end of his string to the doorknob of the closet, pulled it tight, and duct-taped the other end to the floor.

He placed Tink on the bottom of the string. "Now," he whispered. "Go."

Tink looked at him.

"Up."

Her head tilted.

"Up the string. Just hold on and scoot up to the top, as fast as you can."

She looked to the right, then to the left.

"No cat." Ellis crossed his heart and held up his hand. "I promise."

Tink hugged the string and looked around, but she didn't move.

"You are in my power," Ellis whispered. He rolled his eyes around in a circular motion as if he was trying to put her in a trance. "You feel a need to climb this string."

Tink's body jiggled. Ellis could swear she was laughing at him.

"Not you, too." He sank down on the floor and slumped against his closet door. "You and every kid at school think I'm a laugh-riot. Look," he said, "I'm not trying to be funny. Not now, anyway. This is serious. Please climb."

Tink swung the top half of her body away from the string and looked down, as if she might be afraid of heights.

Ellis's words surged straight up from his heart. "Tink. You've *got* to learn to crawl up this string. It's the only way I can help my dad."

Tink bobbed her head, then inched up the string.

"Yes!" exclaimed Ellis. "That's it!" He tried to high-five one of her little legs with his pinky.

She froze.

"Sorry," whispered Ellis. He hummed her favorite marching song.

The good news was that Tink inched farther up the string. The bad news was that he'd seen molasses drip faster than she was moving.

"Uh, Tink," he asked nicely, "could you speed it up a little?"

She continued her steady crawl toward the top.

Ellis couldn't believe his rotten luck. He actually had a woolly worm that was finally doing what he asked, and she was too slow. He shook his head. If all the woolly worms in the forest got together and formed two teams for a foot race, Tink would be the last one picked.

Ellis wondered if Mrs. Puckett had this problem with horses. What would she do? He'd seen dog trainers use treats.

He didn't have any woolly worm treats. He'd already

given her grass and leaves. Mr. Beamer said she liked violets. And lamb's-quarter—whatever that was.

Maybe he could find some violets. Ellis knew that wildflowers grew near the pond, but most of them bloomed in the spring. This was fall. He decided to look anyway. He'd take Tink—maybe fresh air would make her feel zippier.

Gently, Ellis plucked Tink from the string and carried her to the kitchen, where he grabbed a fistful of cereal for the ducks. "Back later," he called to Dad, banging the screen door behind him.

Tink uncurled in his palm. He placed her on his shoulder. She grabbed hold of his shirt with all her feet and looked in every direction.

"No cat," Ellis reassured her.

He strolled down the path past the barn and toward the woods. All along the way, he kept an eye out for violets.

And then he saw the foxes, Socks and Scar. They were trotting down the path ahead of him. He stopped dead-still and watched until they slipped into the woods. They vanished so completely that they could've been ghosts.

He walked quickly then, whistling "Zip-a-Dee-Doo-Dah" and thinking of the words to the song in his head. When he got to the "Mr. Bluebird" part, he substituted

"Miss Woolly Worm's on my shoulder," and he laughed out loud.

Tink held on and swayed to the music.

When they got to the pond, Ellis didn't see a single violet. He didn't see any ducks either. "Puddle!" he called.

Ellis settled onto his rock, just inside the trees. He placed Tink on the mossy part. "This is home," said Ellis. "Remember?"

Tink crawled across the rock, twisting her head left and right. Ellis thought maybe she showed a little extra spring in her step. He congratulated himself for making her happy, and scanned the woods for violets.

Puddle swam around a corner of the pond. One of her babies paddled close behind. A big V rippled behind Puddle. A little V rippled behind her baby. Ellis waited to see ten more little V's cruise around the corner.

He waited some more.

No more ducks.

Just the two.

Where were the babies? Ellis wanted to tell them about Tink. He wanted to introduce them—but from a distance, just in case they thought Tink looked like a Cheerio with fuzz.

Ellis placed Tink back on his shoulder and got up from his rock. He dug into his pocket for cereal.

Puddle swam in the other direction.

That was weird. She never did that.

"Hold on tight," he told Tink. Then he pitched a few Cheerios into the water. Puddle scooted away. Her baby stuck so close to her side she could've been a bandage.

"Supper!" Ellis called after them. "Chow time. Come and get it!"

They swam even farther away. What was the matter with them?

He reached down to pick up some Cheerios that had spilled out of his pocket. And then he saw them. Feathers.

Piles of tiny feathers.

Lots of them.

Ellis felt the blood rush straight up from his heart and into his head. It pounded the space between his ears like a pulse that was bigger than the mountain.

Something had killed his ducks.

Ellis ran all the way home. He pulled on the screen door. It stuck. He pushed on the screen so hard it ripped. He rushed inside. The door slammed behind him. "Mom! Dad!"

"She's not home yet," Dad answered.

"Something killed my ducks!" Ellis shouted.

Dad pushed the lever on his recliner and sat upright. "What?"

Ellis told his dad what happened—what he'd found.

"That's terrible," said Dad. "Maybe a hawk got them. Did you see any—?"

"I saw Socks and Scar."

"The foxes." Dad breathed the words out softly. "Of course."

"I hate them," said Ellis.

Dad looked at him. "It's what foxes do," he said gently.

"I know." Ellis bit his lip so hard, it hurt.

He *did* know. He lived on a mountain. Wildlife was everywhere. He read animal books. He watched nature shows. Animals had to eat. They ate each other.

"Son," said Dad, "I'm sorry."

"Ellis," said Dad, pointing. "There's a woolly worm on your shoulder."

Tink! Tink was hanging upside down, holding on to his shirt with a third of her feet.

Ellis plucked her the rest of the way off. "I forgot you."
He wondered if woolly worms threw up—Tink looked
really wobbly. "I'm sorry."

"Is that the caterpillar you found?"

"Yes."

"You okay?"

"No," said Ellis.

"I'm sorry, Son."

"Me, too," said Ellis.

Ellis took Tink and plodded back up to his room.

How could Puddle let ten of her children get eaten by
foxes? *Ten!* Where had she been when they needed her?

"What a terrible mom," he said out loud.

Tink looked at Ellis. Her fuzzy face was nothing but
two shiny black eyes the size of pin heads, but somehow
they looked sympathetic. Maybe it was the tilt of her head.

"I'd never let that happen to you," said Ellis.

Tink wrapped her prickly self around Ellis's finger. A
hug.

"Thanks," said Ellis.

He cleaned her box, then placed her gently inside it.
Next he sprawled across his bed and punched his pillow.
Ellis swallowed hard to fight the ache in his throat that
meant he might be about to cry.

No ducks. No violets.

But he still had Tink. And violets might make her faster. He'd keep trying.

He heard a soft *tap, tap* on his door.

"Ellie? Baby? Can I come in?"

"Okay," he answered.

Mom slipped into the room and sat down on the side of his bed. She pushed his hair back and said, "I'm really sorry about your ducklings."

"It's okay," said Ellis, taking a deep breath. "That's what foxes do."

"I know," she said, her voice sounding tired and all used up. She stroked the side of his face with one finger. "But I know how much you'll miss them."

Ellis nodded. He *would* miss them.

Mom leaned in closer and hugged him on top of the covers. Ellis reached up and hugged her back. He missed her, too. And Dad. And everything the way it used to be.

14 VIOLETS FOR VICTORY

At school the next day, kids held up their fingers like woolly worms and talked to them. Nobody was being mean—except maybe Randy. Everyone just thought Ellis had meant to be funny.

Ellis felt as if he was carrying a cinderblock on his back, but he didn't know how to fix it. So he just fake-laughed with them. Mostly, he tried to ignore them. He had bigger things to worry about. Like his dad. And the race. Tink was nowhere near ready to race.

Ellis opened his bagged lunch and looked for a place to sit where he could be by himself and think. Tink needed to climb a lot faster. *Would* violets help? Maybe grass and leaves to Tink were like blueberries to Ellis. Tasty, but something new would be a real treat.

"Hey," called George, "Over here." He motioned for Ellis to sit at his lunch table. Ellis hesitated, then slid in next to George, across from Molly and Alice.

Ellis unwrapped his blueberry bread. "Anybody know where I can find violets?"

"Violets?" all three of them asked together.

"Woolly worms eat violets," explained Ellis.

Alice nodded thoughtfully. George and Molly laughed.

Geez. Didn't they know that sometimes he was serious? What if he'd told them about his ducks? They'd probably think he was making a dead-as-a-duck joke.

"Woolly worms like lamb's-quarter, too," said Alice.

Ellis stared at her as if she'd just said, "I found a thousand dollars. Do you want it?"

"You *know* what lamb's-quarter is?"

"Sure," said Alice. She took a bite of her egg salad sandwich.

"Do you know where I can find some?"

"No. Sorry." Alice shook her head. "But Gloria Wilcox has violets blooming in her window box."

"Aunt Glory?" asked Ellis.

Gloria Wilcox wasn't really his aunt. She was a good friend of his mom's who'd asked Ellis to call her Aunt Glory. His parents bought all their cream from the

Wilcoxes because they had Jersey cows, and their cream made the best butter.

Ellis pictured her window boxes. He remembered seeing them when he and Mom took blueberry bread to cheer up Mr. Wilcox after he had fallen off a ladder. He'd broken his arm so badly that the bone stuck out.

"Anybody want Cheetos?" asked Molly, holding open a bag of orange cheese puffs.

Ellis reached in and took a few, wondering how he could get to Aunt Glory's house. It was too far to walk from his house. It was close to school, though—barely a mile.

"You could walk to her house after school," said Alice.

"We'll go with you!" cried Molly,

Ellis shook his head. "I'd miss the bus." He took another handful of cheese puffs. His taste buds were thrilled to be eating something that wasn't blue.

"My dad'll take you home," said George.

Ellis shook his head again. "I've got to do chores."

"Oh, come on," huffed Molly, "there's no rule that says you *have* to do chores."

"Actually," said Ellis, "there is."

Alice leaned forward and echoed Mr. Turnmire, "Never take yourself so seriously you can't make exceptions to your rules."

"Chores," answered Ellis, "are not *my* rules."

"Fine," said Alice. "Then don't take yourself so seriously you can't make exceptions to your *parents'* rules."

"Yeah," said George

"Right," agreed Molly.

Ellis glanced down at his hands. His fingertips weren't blue anymore. The food dye from the orange Cheetos had turned them sort of a gross brown color.

"Look," he said, holding up his fingers. "Show and tell. Orange and blue makes brown."

They all laughed.

"So," said George. "What about it? After school?"

"Come on," Alice urged.

Ellis licked the orange off his fingers.

They were right. It was time to make an exception.

It took them only fifteen minutes to walk to Aunt Glory's. Ellis spotted the violets as soon as he turned up the path to her house. They were sitting in freshly painted white window boxes on either side of her front door. Ellis eyed the flowers as if they were made of gold.

"Wait here," he said. "I'll be right back."

He wondered if he should tell Aunt Glory why he wanted them. She might not give them to him if she knew a bug was going to eat them. Maybe he ought to tell her that he planned to put them in a vase and give them to his mother.

But lying made Ellis nervous. He was sure it was one of the "shalt-not" commandments. Besides, once a lie started, it grew. You had to make up new lies to prop up the old ones, and then all of them got mixed up and paradoxical.

Paradoxical was a Mr. Turnmire vocabulary word. It meant your facts didn't match up, and before you knew it, you were grounded.

It was better to stick to the truth. Well . . . maybe not the whole truth. When he'd called Dad, Ellis had told him he needed to stay after school today. He just hadn't said why.

"You in trouble?" he'd asked.

"No."

"Got a ride home?"

"Yes."

"Who's driving?"

"Mr. Johnson."

"What about your chores?"

"I'll do them." Ellis didn't know when, but Dad hadn't asked when.

"I don't know, Ellis. Your mother—"

"Dad," Ellis begged.

"Okay."

Ellis hadn't lied, but he knew Dad thought his staying had something to do with school, not violets. If Aunt Glory assumed her violets were headed for a crystal vase, Ellis figured there was no need to tell her they were destined for a worm's butt.

Maybe she wouldn't even care. When she answered the door, Ellis was reminded that she wasn't really the crystal-vase type. She had on dirty jeans and a baggy shirt. Her boots were covered with barn muck from milking her cows.

"Violets?" she asked. "Sure, Ellis. Pick as many as you want." She looked over his head at the three friends waiting by her mailbox, raised an eyebrow, and grinned. "They for your girlfriend?"

Ellis's brain thought fast. "Yes, ma'am."

"What's her name?" asked Aunt Glory.

"Tink," he answered, reaching into one of the window boxes and plucking three violets.

"Cute name."

"Yes, ma'am."

"She from around here?" Aunt Glory strained to get a closer look at Molly and Alice.

"We just met," said Ellis, continuing to pick.

"I'm so glad you have friends," said Aunt Glory. "I worry about a young boy like you—alone and working so much. How's your dad?"

"Not bad."

"Your mom hasn't been by to buy any cream lately."

"She's real busy," said Ellis.

"Wait here." Aunt Glory went inside and came back holding a glass jar half-full of thick milky liquid and handed it to Ellis.

Ellis froze. If he left with flowers *and* cream, they'd be big-time beholden. Plus, Mom would have to find time to churn the cream into butter.

"No thanks," said Ellis. "I'd better not."

"Don't be silly." Aunt Glory put the jar in his hands and wrapped her hands tight around his. "It's a gift."

"But—"

"No buts."

Ellis had a feeling that if he said no again, she'd lock the jar around his neck with a bike chain. Aunt Glory was a tough person to say no to, so he took it.

"Aunt Glory?"

"Mmm?"

"Could *I* make butter?"

"Honey, *anybody* can make butter. Do you want to do

it the wear-yourself-out way with a wooden churn, or the fun way?"

"There's a fun way?"

"Of course," said Aunt Glory. "You and your friends pass this jar around. Take turns shaking it. Before you know it, it'll be butter."

"I didn't know you could do that," said Ellis. He looked doubtfully at the creamy liquid and tried to imagine shaking it solid.

"The afternoon knows what the morning never expected," said Aunt Glory.

"Huh?" answered Ellis. Aunt Glory was full of snappy sayings that made him think too hard. "Butter? Really?"

Aunt Glory put her hands on her hips. "I don't lie."

"No." That was a fact. Aunt Glory never lied.

She looked down at Ellis and recited, "A whispered lie is just as wrong as one that's thundered loud and long."

Ellis didn't want to say "huh" again, so he said, "Yes, ma'am."

"Now git." She motioned her arms to shoo Ellis off her porch.

Ellis hurried up her walk, waving good-bye with the hand clutching the violets. His other hand carried the cream jar. "Thanks," he called back.

Aunt Glory threw him a kiss. "I hope your girlfriend likes the violets."

"Your girlfriend?" Molly exclaimed as Ellis rejoined them.

"She means Tink," Ellis explained.

George's eyes widened. "You told Mrs. Wilcox your girlfriend was a woolly worm?"

"Not exactly."

"What's in the jar?" asked Alice.

"Cream," said Ellis. "To make butter."

"For your girlfriend?" George drawled out "girlfriend" so that it had enough syllables to be one of Mr. Turnmire's vocabulary words.

"No. For my mom."

"That's nice," said Alice.

"Show us the violets," said Molly.

Ellis held up his fistful of flowers.

"I hope Tink likes them," said Alice.

"Yeah," said Ellis, taking a deep breath. "Me, too." He slid them into his pocket and shook the cream as they walked. At first he just jiggled it. Then he began to shake the jar as if he were trying to kill it. *Slap-sloosh-slap-sloosh.*

"Aunt Glory says if we shake it, it'll turn into butter," he said. "But my arms are about to break and nothing's happening."

He passed it to George. "Shake it! Quick. Keep it going."

George jiggled it, looking at Ellis and asking, "Why am I doing this?"

"Because my mother loves homemade butter. Come on. Shake harder!"

"That looks a lot like work," said Molly.

Alice took the jar from George and shook it.

"Thanks," said Ellis.

"Sure," answered Alice.

Alice pumped the jar with one hand, then switched to the other. When that arm slowed down, George stepped in and took a turn.

Ellis, Molly, George, and Alice passed it and shook, passed it and shook, as they walked toward the park where George's dad would pick them up.

But the cream stayed liquid.

"Don't give up," said Ellis. "Quitters never win and winners never quit."

"Oh, please," Molly groaned. "You sound like Mrs. Wilcox."

"My arm is dying," moaned George.

"It's not working," said Alice.

And then, as Ellis suddenly wondered if Aunt Glory

really was a liar, the cream looked thicker. "Hey!" he shouted. "It *is* working."

With a burst of energy, they all passed it around again.

"Look!" yelled Molly, holding up the jar.

"It's butter!" cheered Alice.

Ellis's smile covered his whole face.

Turning the corner, he saw the creek with three girls and a big black dog splashing in it. Beyond that, more kids played on the park's slides and swings.

Ellis had butter for Mom and violets for Tink. *And* he was headed to the park with his friends.

As they ran closer, George spotted a ball in the grassy open space. He raced forward, scooped it up, and yelled, "Catch!"

Ellis set down the butter jar, caught the ball, then tossed it to Alice.

Randy appeared out of nowhere and snatched it out of Alice's hands. He held it high in the air. "You can't reach it!" he taunted.

George rushed him, tackling him to the ground. As Randy tried to get up and run, George grabbed his foot and held on. Randy dragged him through the grass. George yanked Randy's shoe off and held it up like a prize.

"Give me back my shoe!" shouted Randy.

George threw it to Molly.

"Yes!" she yelled, lobbing it straight to Alice. "Keep away!"

Randy lunged toward Alice, arms stretched out to tackle her. She sidestepped and tossed the shoe to Ellis.

Ellis caught it and held it up to his face. He stuck his nose right down in it and faked a huge whiff of shoe stink. He gasped, gagged, and dropped the shoe. He swayed back and forth. With one hand he gripped his throat. His other hand grabbed his chest, and he dropped down dead.

"Very funny," said Randy, picking up his shoe.

Ellis grinned. It *was* funny.

George high-fived Ellis.

Randy grabbed Ellis's butter jar and shouted, "Keep away!" He tossed it to George who was standing at the edge of the creek bank. George missed the catch, his hands scrambling in the empty air. The jar fell and shattered on a rock.

Ellis watched helplessly as the fistful of butter bobbed up in the creek like a giant yellow cork and floated down the stream.

"You are such a jerk!" George shouted at Randy.

Randy froze, a look of surprise on his face. Ellis thought Randy was going to apologize. But then he just shrugged and said, "You asked for it. Keep away! Remember?"

"It's not the same!" yelled Molly. "Your smelly old shoe didn't get drowned!"

Ellis watched Mom's butter disappear around a bend in the creek, headed for the Yadkin River and maybe even the Atlantic Ocean.

"I'm really sorry," said Alice, turning toward Ellis.

"No big deal," Ellis answered. But he didn't mean it. For his mom, butter *was* a big deal. He wanted to tackle Randy and shove his face into the dirt.

Randy had a saggy, sick look on his face, as if he really was sorry but still couldn't say it. Molly and George were both waving their arms in his face and telling him what a jerk he was.

Alice touched Ellis's arm sympathetically. He stared at

her hand, surprised. His friends were standing up for him, and he wasn't even being funny.

Ellis felt his anger at Randy shrink from a giant fireball to a tiny match flame that flickered once, twice, then went out.

15 HOME IMPROVE-MENTS

"Thanks for the ride," said Ellis.

"Any time," said Mr. Johnson.

Ellis waved to George and his dad as they disappeared down his dirt drive.

Ellis hurried inside his house. Dad had done two of his chores for him and was heating up chicken noodle soup for dinner, even though his eyes had that pinched I'm-in-pain look.

"Thanks, Dad."

Dad jerked his hand in a way that meant *no problem* and said, "You better start your homework."

Ellis bounded up the stairs to his room and raced down the hall. "Tink!" he shouted, crossing his room in two strides. He lifted the lid from her box. "What's up?"

If a woolly worm could squint, that's what Tink was

doing. For the first time, Ellis realized how dark her box must be with the lid on. It was probably kind of hot, too, even with the airholes.

Tink raised up half her body into the air to greet him.

"My day," said Ellis, "was good and bad."

Tink waited.

"I had a present for Mom, but it got ruined. That's the bad thing." Ellis held Tink up to his face so that they were nose to nose. "But wait'll you see the good thing. Come on, Tink. Guess what I found?"

Tink stared blankly at him. Then her mouth moved a little, as if she were chewing.

"Yes!" Ellis exclaimed, nodding energetically. "Violets." Ellis pulled the flowers out of his pocket. They looked pretty droopy. "I'll put them in water," he said. "Maybe they'll perk up."

Tink stretched herself like an accordion toward the flowers.

"Well," said Ellis, "maybe just one taste. But first, let's clean your castle."

Ellis dumped the frass out of Tink's box, and then set her back in it with one floppy violet. Tink's nose wiggled. At least Ellis thought it wiggled. He couldn't actually *see* a nose, but her prickly hairs made a twitchy move, so there must be one in there somewhere. And then she was on the violet like a fly on cheese.

While she munched away, Ellis stuck the rest of the violets in a glass with water. Tink didn't like to be watched while she ate, so he opened his bear book to read about Kodiak bears—like the one on his postcard. He read aloud to her—all about how big the bears were and how they lived in Alaska and how they caught salmon with their paws.

And then Ellis read something amazing. When they hibernated, they didn't poop. They magically formed some sort of a plug—like a cork, only it was probably made of the vegetables they ate. It kept them from making a mess in their dens while they slept all winter.

"You need one of those," he told Tink.

She continued to eat.

"That's enough for now." Ellis reached in and pulled what was left of the violet away from Tink.

Her neck stretched to follow it.

"Don't worry," said Ellis. "You can get it back." He plucked her out of the box and placed her on her string racetrack. He attached the violet to the top of the string. "Go," he whispered.

Tink grabbed hold. She looked at him.

He moved the violet and held it lower—just above her nose.

Tink wiggled her nose and got a whiff of the flower. She began to crawl, slowly. Ellis moved the violet a little higher. She sped up. Ellis moved it to the top of the string.

The promise of that violet sent Tink into a sprint. Her multiple tiny legs gripped and pumped like pistons. She reached the top in twenty seconds.

For a caterpillar, that was a hundred miles an hour.

Ellis yelled, "You did it!" He dropped the violet and patted her. It felt like stroking an old toothbrush with worn out bristles. He praised her. He hugged her with one finger. He kissed her. The fuzz tickled his lips.

Tink swiveled the upper half of her body up and away as if to say, "Where's the violet?"

Ellis swung her around in the air as if he had a tiny dance partner in his arms. Then he gently placed her back in her box and dropped the violet in after her. Tink scurried over to it and buried her face straight into one of the petals.

Ellis's insides were doing jumping jacks. "You're fast! You listened! You're going to win a thousand dollars for Dad!"

Ellis wanted to reward her—something besides violets. He needed to save those.

Ellis looked at her box. It was dark. And probably stuffy, too. Tink deserved better. Her castle needed home improvements.

Ellis closed the lid and whispered, "Wait here."

In five minutes he was back with a piece of screen Dad had left over from fixing the kitchen door Ellis had ripped. He cut it to fit across the top of her box, then folded the edges over so she couldn't push it off. Now she had more air and light.

Tink was still eating her violet. Ellis couldn't see any munch or hear any crunch, but her face was moving steadily through the flower, which was slowly vanishing one petal at a time.

"Do you like your new box top?" he asked.

Tink lifted her head just enough for a quick head bob, then thrust it back into the violet.

"You're welcome," said Ellis. Then he looked at the rest of the saggy flowers in the water glass. They had to stay alive until Saturday. Everything depended on them.

After dinner, he gave her another sniff of violet, then attached it to the top of the string. Tink went after it like a cheetah chasing a gazelle. Every time she reached the top, she ate. Ellis tried not to think about how much frass there'd be.

The next morning, Ellis woke up early to race Tink. He wanted to be sure he hadn't just dreamed she was faster than lightning.

The flowers in the water glass had perked up like new.

The frass in the box was knee-deep.

Ellis placed Tink on her string and attached a violet. She zipped to the top in nineteen seconds.

Ellis stroked the top of her fuzzy head. "You're even faster," he exclaimed. "That was your personal best!"

Tink chewed on her violet.

"We can't lose!"

Tink kept chewing, but Ellis thought he saw a hiccup head bob.

He wished he could take her outside as a reward—maybe back to the pond where she could feel at home—but he didn't have time. He'd miss his bus.

Ellis cleaned her box. Then he glanced around his room, looking for the best place to put it.

"No more stuffy days for you," he said, opening his window and placing her box in front of it. He made sure the screen lid was tight. Then he positioned it where it would stay in the shade.

He didn't want to come home and find cooked caterpillar.

"Better?" he asked.

She rippled her body in a way that looked happy. Then she stretched her body up, sniffing for another violet.

Ellis counted to make sure he had enough to last until the race, and handed her one. He couldn't see her mouth, but he didn't have to. He knew it was smiling.

At school Ellis tried to go unnoticed. For one whole day, he would not be the class funny guy. He had two good reasons.

One—talking caterpillar jokes weren't funny. He had

130

the winning woolly worm, and he wanted to lay low until he could prove it.

Two—he hadn't done his homework. He had meant to. He really had. But he'd forgotten.

All morning, he acted invisible.

When Alice asked him if Tink had liked the violets, Ellis nodded enthusiastically, then buried his face in his math book.

When Molly asked him if he'd told his mother about the butter, he shook his head no, and then he got up to sharpen his pencil.

When George challenged him to a burping contest, he claimed his throat hurt.

When Mr. Turnmire asked for his homework, Ellis pretended he hadn't heard him.

"Maybe his talking woolly worm ate it," said Randy. "The very hungry caterpillar." He could barely get it out, he was laughing so hard.

Ellis had to admit, it was funny. Or at least, it would have been if *he'd* said it.

"Ellis," Mr. Turnmire repeated.

He knew he had to say something, so finally, he answered, "I'm sorry, Mr. Turnmire. I didn't have time to do it."

Mr. Turnmire looked disappointed. Part of Ellis felt terrible—he hated to let Mr. Turnmire down. But the other half of him didn't care—he couldn't wait to get back to Tink.

Ellis ran up his driveway after the bus dropped him off. He grabbed some green leaves for Tink and dashed through the kitchen door. It slammed behind him.

"I'm home!" he called to Dad, then raced up the stairs.

"I'm home!" he repeated to Tink as he flung open the door to his room. "Are you ready to race?"

Ellis's room was small, and there wasn't much in it. He could see everything there was to see in one glance.

Tink's box was turned on its side. The screen lid was off.

Frass spilled onto the floor along with her spongy limb, three twigs, and her mossy rock. Tink was not there.

But Ginger, the cat, was. She was curled up on his bed, fast asleep.

16 GONE

Tink was gone.

Ellis shoved Ginger out of his window and practically slammed it on her tail.

Frantically, he looked everywhere—under his bed, outside the window, between his sheets, in the closet, all through his toy chest. But he knew where Tink was. She was in Ginger's stomach.

He didn't come out of his room until dinnertime. He tossed Tink's branch, twigs, and rocks back into her box and shoved it under his bed. Then he swept up the frass and some mystery dirt that had appeared out of nowhere and pitched all of it out the window.

He flopped onto his bed. No thousand dollars. No surgery. No Tink. His small room felt huge and empty.

When Ellis finally came downstairs, Dad was putting

supper on the table. He'd heated up a can of baked beans and microwaved four sausage biscuits from the freezer. He felt Ellis's forehead.

"You sick?"

"No."

"What's wrong?"

"Tink's gone."

"Your woolly worm?"

"Yes, sir."

"Lost?"

"Maybe."

"Dead?"

"Probably."

Dad pulled up a chair. "I'll bet you can find another one."

Ellis blinked to keep his eyes from filling up. "No thanks." He was glad Dad hadn't known about his plan to win a thousand dollars.

Ellis took a bite of biscuit, but halfway down his throat, the sausage hit a logjam of acid and spurted back up. He reswallowed. It burned.

After that, Ellis just pushed the beans around on his plate and tried not to throw up in his mouth again.

"Tomorrow's Thursday," said Dad.

"I know."

"Woolly Worm Festival's Saturday."

"Yeah," Ellis nodded.

"You know what that means."

Ellis knew exactly what it meant. It meant he didn't have a caterpillar for the race, and it was too late to train another one. Besides, he didn't want another one. He wanted Tink.

"It means there's a lot of work to be done around here," said Dad.

"Yeah." Ellis knew that too. His mom would have a million jobs for him.

"You're a good helper," said Dad, standing and squeezing Ellis's shoulder. "I don't know what your Mom and I would do without you."

Wow, thought Ellis. That was a lot of words for Dad.

"Thanks, Dad," said Ellis. He got up, cleared the table, and began to wash the dishes. He made too many suds and turned the water extra hot. He thrust his hands into the fiery dishwater as if it were a punishment.

When Mom got home, Ellis was in bed. She knocked on his door. He closed his eyes and pretended to be asleep.

* * *

The next morning, Ellis stayed in bed. Mom had to call him to breakfast four times.

"What's wrong?" she asked when he finally came downstairs. "Are you still upset about your ducks?"

"And my woolly worm," said Ellis.

"You had a woolly worm?" asked Mom.

"Yes, I had a woolly worm!" Ellis shouted. "You don't remember?"

Mom reached over and touched his arm. "Ellie. Baby. I'm sorry. I just forgot. What happened?"

"The cat ate it."

Mom sighed. "I knew having that cat around was trouble."

"Mom!"

"I'm sorry. But, Ellis, these things happen. Then life goes on. Just remember, God never gives us more than we can bear." She squeezed his hand.

"Mom," said Ellis, "I don't want to talk about it."

"But—"

"Please."

"All right." She ruffled his hair. "I've got to go. You have a good day at school. Try not to think about your caterpillar." She grabbed her purse, then turned. "Don't forget, when you get home from school, we have *lots* to do. The Woolly Worm Festival is the day after tomorrow."

"I know," said Ellis.

Mom blew him a kiss and hurried off to work.

At school, Alice, George, and Molly met him at the front door.

"How's Tink?" asked Alice.

"Dead," said Ellis.

Molly scrunched her eyebrows together and looked at Ellis as if she was waiting for the punch line.

"I don't think he's joking," said George.

"Me either," said Alice.

Molly gaped at Ellis. He watched her blink about a thousand times while she considered the fact that he might be telling the truth—that not everything he said was a joke.

Ellis walked away.

In class, he was so quiet, Mr. Turnmire sent him to see the school nurse. Ellis lay down on the cot in the sickroom and stayed there all day. That way, he didn't have to talk to anyone about anything.

After school, he helped his mom prepare for her booth at the Woolly Worm Festival. She was planning to sell a ton of blueberry stuff there. She'd even taken off Thursday afternoon and all day Friday from work to get ready.

Ellis sat at the kitchen table and sifted through the blueberries he'd washed. If he saw a stem still attached, he plucked it off. Then he measured about a million one cup batches for Mom to fold into her batter. He poured the batter into muffin tins and put them in the oven while Mom started mixing another batch from scratch.

He rolled out pie crusts for Mom's blueberry pies. She draped them into pie pans and crimped the crusts so they looked wavy. Ellis tried to crimp a crust, but it ended up looking like shredded wheat.

"Let's keep that pie for ourselves," said Mom.

All the yummy bakery smells had made Ellis's mouth water, so, as soon as the messed up pie cooked, Ellis cut a piece and ate it before Mom could change her mind. He took a bigger slice to Dad.

He measured out milk, flour, and sugar. He poured bread batter into loaf pans and wondered if he should write an obituary for Tink.

Tink was a good friend and a terrific caterpillar.

He washed cake and pie pans, muffin tins, wooden stirring spoons, measuring cups, and whisks.

She had a sense of humor.

He placed baked stuff on racks to cool.

She loved music and violets.

More warm sugary aromas filled the house, drifted out the windows, and floated over the mountains.

If she'd lived, she would have won a thousand dollars for Ellis Coffey's dad.

Friday was a teacher workday. No school. Ellis wrapped all the bread loaves and muffins in clear wrap and labeled them. He put the pies and cakes in individual boxes. He loaded cases of jam into Mom's truck. He couldn't stop thinking about Tink.

He decided to walk to the pond.

As he walked, he found himself hoping Tink would be there waiting, or racing across a rock, bobbing her head like a hiccup. He walked slowly, scanning the path, looking down under rocks and leaves, staring up at tree trunks.

What if Ginger hadn't eaten Tink? What if Tink had escaped and crawled back to where she lived in the woods? Miracles happened in the Bible. Why not in Banner Elk?

When he got to the pond, he settled onto his rock and called, "Tink! Are you here? Do you copy?"

Nothing.

"I have a violet." Ellis held a purple flower in the air and waved it back and forth.

Still nothing. Just some bird twitters and a tiny breeze making the leaves crinkle. He sang three verses of "Onward, Christian Soldiers."

Puddle and her baby glided across the pond.

Ellis looked at Puddle and said, "I'm sorry I got mad at you for not protecting your babies."

Puddle swam in a slow circle, her baby next to her.

He watched and waited until the sun began to set and the dark shadows stretched out like ghosts. And then he went home, alone.

17 ALICE'S CATERPILLAR COLLECTION

Ellis stood under a small rented tent space at the Woolly Worm Festival, helping his mom sell blueberry stuff: jam, cakes, pies, breads, muffins. Ellis thought if she could find a way to make pencils out of blueberries, they'd be selling those, too.

The air smelled like onions, Italian sausages, and sugar. People were everywhere—half of them munching hot dogs, caramel apples, and funnel cakes. Kids jumped up and down in inflatable bouncy houses. Grown-ups shopped at the craft booths. Moms and dads clutched the hands of little kids so they didn't lose them. A loudspeaker blared nonstop, broadcasting the caterpillar races.

"*Whoa!*" shouted the man with the microphone. The PA system made that piercing, screechy sound. "Would you look at Wiggle!" he yelled. "The worm in lane number three is going backward! Sea Biscuit's standing still! But Lightning's coming on fast. It's a two-worm race! Lightning in lane nine—Wascal in lane twenty-three. It's close. It's really close!" *Tweet!* he blew his whistle. "We've got a winner!"

Ellis tried not to listen. He focused on selling their blueberry stuff—fast—so he could go home. But they had a hundred jars of jam, twenty cakes, thirty pies, forty loaves of bread, and a million muffins.

The sun was out and so warm he wore a short-sleeved shirt. Not like last year when he needed a jacket. In October, Banner Elk weather could be beach-day or blizzard. Ellis thought Tink would have loved to be outside on a day this nice.

Ellis glanced up and saw Alice. She carried a cardboard box way out in front of her like she was a page delivering a king's crown on a pillow. George and Molly walked beside her.

Alice set the box on the table and said, "Surprise!"

"Surprise?"

The box crawled with woolly worms. At least a dozen wiggled their way between leaves and sticks.

"You're selling woolly worms," said Ellis. "Good idea." He wished he'd thought of it. Lots of kids collected them

the week before the festival and sold them for five dollars
each. But Ellis had been too busy dreaming of a thousand
dollars to bother with anything smaller.

"They're not for sale." Alice pointed to the worms.
"They're for you."

"Huh?"

We found them at the park after school," said Alice. "I
know none of them are Tink, but we wanted to help."

"You can race one of these," said Molly.

"Yeah," said George. "Pick one." He had powdered
sugar on his nose from eating a funnel cake.

Ellis waited to see if they were going to make a joke
about talking caterpillars. When they didn't, he said,
"Thanks, but I can't race. I have to help Mom."

Molly slammed her fists on her hips and said, "Ellis!
Take a break."

George and Alice nodded in agreement.

"I don't have time to train one," said Ellis.

"So," said George. "You don't have to win. Do it for fun."

"You don't understand," said Ellis.

"Don't understand what?" asked George.

And before Ellis could think about what he was saying, he blurted out everything. He told them he *did* have to win. His dad needed an operation. The deductible cost a thousand dollars, and he was a worm whisperer—at least maybe he was—and it wasn't funny.

George, Molly, and Alice stared at him. Then Molly jammed her hands back on her hips again and said, "Okay. Here's the plan. You sell all these woolly worms but one. That one you race. Since you're a worm whisperer, you win the thousand dollars. No joke." She spread her palms just below shoulder height. "Add it to the profits from selling the other caterpillars and there you have it. One back surgery with money left over."

Alice and George nodded in agreement.

"It's not that simple," said Ellis.

"Why not?" said Alice.

"Even a worm whisperer has to have a caterpillar he knows. It takes time."

"Well," said Alice, "Sell these. You could make *some* money."

"Ellis!" Mom called. She had a line of customers waiting to pay.

"I have to go," said Ellis.

"Okay," said Molly, "but keep the worms." She dragged George off by the hand. Alice said, "Good luck," and followed them.

Ellis watched them go. He had spilled his guts, and they hadn't laughed. They'd tried to help.

"Ellis!" Mom called again.

He placed the box under the table where it would be out of the way and hurried over to make change for people. In between customers, he stared at the caterpillars. Maybe he should try.

He picked up one that looked sort of like Tink except she had two more dark fuzzy bands than Tink had had.

She curled up in a ball in his hand.

"Hey," he whispered. "Ellis to woolly worm. Do you copy?

Nothing. No smile. No head bob.

"Hey you!" he yelled. "Wake up!"

"It's not only what you say, it's how you say it," said a voice so smooth it flowed like water.

Ellis looked up and saw Mrs. Puckett, the horse whisperer. She reached down and took the caterpillar out of Ellis's hand and said something so soft and convincing it made Ellis want to do whatever she said. And he wasn't even a horse.

The caterpillar uncurled and raised itself up.

"See," said Mrs. Puckett as she handed the caterpillar back to Ellis. She winked at him and disappeared into the crowd.

He lifted the woolly worm up to his face and begged, "Will you help me?" Its black, beady eyes were totally blank. If Ellis did have a gift, *this* worm sure didn't know it.

"That the winning worm?" asked Doc Swenson, ambling over.

"No, sir," said Ellis.

"Looks like a winner to me," said Doc, rubbing one bushy eyebrow. "What're you waiting for? Sign her up."

"Um . . . no money," said Ellis, pulling his pockets inside out as proof. It was true. He didn't have the five dollar entry fee.

"Here." Doc tried to stuff a five-dollar bill into Ellis's shirt pocket. "Pay me back after you win."

"No, sir," said Ellis, backing away. "I can't take that."

Doc laughed. It was a big sound that came up from his

belly. Then he bought a jar of blueberry jam and paid Mom. He refused to take his five dollars in change. "It's a tip," he said. "For Ellis."

Mom tried to hand it back, but Doc had vanished.

She shrugged and handed the money to Ellis.

Ellis held the five-dollar bill open with two hands. The face of Abraham Lincoln looked up at him.

"Should I enter the race?" Ellis asked him.

Lincoln didn't answer.

Ellis shook his head. Not this worm. He placed the woolly worm back in the box. He squatted down next to it. "Ellis to woolly worms. Does anybody copy?"

All of them ignored him.

Ellis felt a sickening twist in his stomach. Just because Mrs. Puckett got through to them, didn't mean Ellis could. Apparently he wasn't a worm whisperer after all.

18 BACK IN BUSINESS

A sharp clap made Ellis jump.

Ellis looked up and discovered the sound had been Miss Bluford clapping for joy at the sight of blueberry bread. She had already placed her tiny dog on the ground, and now she was digging money out of her purse to pay Mom.

Ellis had never seen such a small dog. He thought it possible that a woolly worm could beat it up. But Grace didn't act tiny. Like a hound scenting a raccoon, all four pounds of her went straight for Ellis's caterpillar box. She sniffed it like it was a treasure chest of doggie treats.

"Hey!" shouted Ellis, snatching up the box. "Get away from there!"

Miss Bluford turned. "Ellis! Hello," she greeted him. "What's in the box?"

"Woolly worms," said Ellis, lifting it higher so Grace

couldn't snack on one. "Well," said Miss Bluford. "The last time I saw you, you had only one caterpillar to race. Now you have a dozen. Are you going to race all of them?"

"No, ma'am," said Ellis

"I see," said Miss Bluford. "You're selling them."

"No, ma'am."

But Miss Bluford wasn't listening. She was too busy picking up caterpillars, holding them up to the light, turning them over and examining their squirmy legs. "I'll take this one," she said.

Why not? thought Ellis. "That'll be five dollars."

Miss Bluford paid him for the caterpillar. "I'll name it

Amazing Grace," she said. "After my little Grace here."
She reached down and patted her dog.

Ellis leaned over to scratch Grace behind her ears. Then
he pointed to Amazing Grace and said, "You've got a real
winner there. Better keep it away from your dog."

"My little Grace wouldn't hurt a flea," said Miss Bluford,
scooping her up and introducing her to the new woolly
worm. Grace sniffed Amazing Grace, who curled up into
a ball as Miss Bluford walked away balancing a dog, a
caterpillar, and two loaves of blueberry bread in her arms.

Then, in less time than it takes to eat a funnel cake,
Ellis had sold the entire box of woolly worms. People were
buying them faster than he could count.

When the box was empty, he did count. Twelve woolly
worms at five dollars apiece. That was sixty dollars! He
couldn't believe it. He stared at the money and wished
he'd spent his time collecting caterpillars instead of training Tink.

Mom stared at the money, too. She shook her head and
mumbled something about how long it took to make that
much jam. Ellis wondered if they'd ditch their blueberry
business and raise woolly worms next year.

"How's it going?"

It was Dad, carrying a seat cushion. He'd come to help

out. He placed the pillow on the hard bottom of their folding chair so he'd be more comfortable.

"We should be in the worm business," muttered Mom.

Dad sat on the cushion, put his feet up, and tilted the chair onto its back legs. Ellis wondered how long he'd be able to stay.

"Ellis," he said. "Go find your friends."

Ellis looked at Mom. She nodded.

He found Alice and Molly and George up near the stage, watching the beginning of the next race. It was one of the last heats. Just three more and then the last semifinal race would be run, followed by the finals.

When that was over, the mayor would hold up the winning worm and "read" him. An instant wiggly winter weather report.

"Get your worms ready!" boomed the man with the mike. "In lane number one we have Rocky Top, hailing from Tennessee. Had to cross state lines to get here. How about a round of applause for my man Merlin, in lane number two? Maybe he swam over from England. And in lane three—let's give a warm welcome to Amazing Grace, how sweet she is. In lane number four—"

"Miss Bluford," Ellis shouted, "good luck!"

Then he turned to Alice and said, "Here's your money."

He held the sixty dollars out to her. "This is yours and George's and Molly's."

"No," she said. "It's yours."

"Are you crazy? There's sixty dollars here! You found the worms, not me."

"It's close!" boomed Microphone Man. "It's close! *Tweet!* We haaaave a winner! All right folks, let's hear it for Amazing Grace!"

Ellis looked up at the stage. Miss Bluford had won! She was grinning and clapping her hands so hard Ellis was afraid she might break one. Grace was wagging her tail even faster than Miss Bluford was clapping. Alice and Ellis cheered. George and Molly whooped.

Alice leaned in close to Ellis. "*Are* you a worm whisperer?" she asked.

Ellis shrugged. "I don't know."

"You need to enter the race," said Alice, "and find out."

Ellis hated to waste the money for the entry fee. "Tink was trained," he argued. "She was ready."

"So?" said Alice. "Woolly worms listen to you."

"Some of them do," said Ellis. "Some of them don't."

Alice grabbed Ellis's hand and pulled him over to a little kid sitting cross-legged in front of a bucket. He had a sign taped on it that said

WOOllY WoRms foR SAle. $5.00 EACH.

He glanced up and grinned. "Only two left. You want one?"

"Do it," urged Alice. "Whisper something."

Ellis crouched down next to the box. He felt silly.

"Go on," she said.

"I'm Ellis," he said in his nicest voice. "Do you copy?"

One woolly worm ignored him. The other one twisted toward the sound of Ellis's voice.

Ellis picked up the worm. He placed it in the palm of his hand.

"Crawl across my hand," Ellis whispered in his most convincing voice. "Please."

The woolly worm inched across his palm, circled over to the back of his hand, and crept over his knuckles.

Ellis picked it up and held it directly in front of his face. "I need you to race. You need to be fast."

The caterpillar pumped its legs in the empty air.

Ellis's heart skipped a beat. Was he imagining it, or was this woolly worm listening to him?

What had Mrs. Puckett said? *It's not only what you say, it's how you say it.* Maybe he *could* race a new woolly worm. He remembered what had worked when he'd trained Tink.

To make her understand, he didn't necessarily have to whisper. He just had to be convincing . . . and serious. It had to come from his heart—it had to matter.

Like when he'd told Tink about Dad.

And, Ellis realized with a jolt, like when he'd told his friends.

"Look," said Ellis, holding the caterpillar in front of his eyes. "I have a problem." He inched even closer to the worm, then glanced around to make sure a hundred people weren't watching him. "Actually, it's my dad's problem," he whispered. "But it's messing up my family pretty bad. Are you fast? Can you help?"

The caterpillar did two head bobs.

Ellis's heart almost leaped out of his chest. Quickly, he peeled a five dollar bill out of the sixty-dollar wad and handed the rest to Alice to hold. He gave the five dollars to the boy, held up the woolly worm, and said, "I'll take this one."

Alice, Molly, and George cheered.

Ellis looked past the crowds of people to where his dad was tilted back, sitting on a cushion. Ellis stood straight, clenched his teeth, and puffed out his chest.

I *am* going to win, he thought. I have to.

19 ON YOUR MARK, GET SET, GO!

"Laaaast heat before the laaaast semifinal," blasted the loudspeaker. "Is evvvvvvvverybody ready?"

"Yes!" roared the crowd.

"Zigzag's ready in lane one! Let's hope he can walk a straight string. Pegasus is chomping at the bit in lane two! And let's hear it for Belle in lane number three!"

That's us, thought Ellis as the microphone man continued to announce the other contestants. Me and my new woolly worm. He had named her Belle after Tink—because both names were short for Tinkerbell.

"Go Ellis!" screamed George. "Go Belle!"

"You can do it, you can do it, you can, you can!" Alice and Molly chanted together.

Miss Bluford clapped for joy and cried, "Belle's the best!"

Doc Swenson shouted, "Show 'em no mercy!"

"Ah!" exclaimed the man with the microphone—the funny guy who'd been calling the races all day. He whipped off his cap, which was covered up with fake woolly worms, and waved it in Ellis's direction. "There's a local favorite in lane three!"

Ellis's heart felt as if it was being gripped by a fist. Everyone he knew was watching him. Belle was a stranger. He didn't have a single violet. He didn't know if she liked music. It was all up to his worm whispering.

For the mere ten minutes he'd known Belle, he'd done nothing but chant, "You have to climb up, and you have to climb fast. Do it for me. Do it for Dad." Over and over. He'd said it like it was the most important thing in the world—because it was.

She seemed pretty twitchy, so maybe it was working.

In fact, she was acting exactly like Chester, sprinting from one knuckle to the next, onto his palm, up his arm, over his shoulder.

But Chester lost, thought Ellis. No problem, he told himself. It's not the same. That was last year. This year, I'm a worm whisperer.

He plucked her off of his back and said, "Not yet. Chill out."

He checked out the other caterpillar contestants.

Zigzag, Pegasus, Woolly Wonka, Frostbite, Dr. Pepper. And nineteen more.

None of them were zipping around like Belle.

"You," he whispered into her fuzz, "are a winner."

She stretched the top half of her body toward the string. Reaching. Ready to go.

He nudged her with his thumb. "Easy girl." He used his calm voice. "You have to wait."

Ellis placed her back on his shoulder, because that's where Tink liked to sit. "Stay," he whispered.

She didn't. Tiny feet pinpricked up onto his neck, across his shoulder, then down his back.

Ellis couldn't reach her. He twisted his left arm up the middle of his back. He twisted his right arm over his left shoulder. He tried to nab her as she scooted between his shoulder blades. He knew he looked like a pretzel.

All he grabbed was shirt. "Hey!" he cried. "Where are you?"

"It seems that Ellis Coffey," said Microphone Man, "has lost control of his worm."

The people in the crowd laughed. Then, for some reason, they laughed even louder.

Ellis twisted his head sideways to see what else was so funny. And there was Belle. On his back. Speeding south.

He couldn't reach her. Then, he couldn't even see her. Suddenly she was on his butt. He tried to snatch her up, but she gripped his pants as if she had glue on her feet. Ellis tugged harder. Finally she let go.

He held her in front of his face and frowned.

The crowd was laughing so hard that they drowned out Microphone Man.

Ellis grinned a goofy grin. He was on a stage. Making people laugh. It felt kind of good. Maybe he should do something funnier.

No, he thought. That was stupid. The race was serious. He didn't always have to be funny.

"On your mark!" shouted the man with the mike.

Ellis placed Belle on the string.

"Get set!"

She hugged the string with all her feet.

"Go!"

Ellis released her.

"You have to climb *up*, and you have to climb *fast*," he urged.

She started to climb. Not super fast, but steady. Up. Up. Up. She rippled as she rose. Her little pink feet grabbed and pulled, grabbed and pulled.

"Belle is off and running!" shouted Microphone Man. "But Zigzag is gaining. Pegasus is frozen. Hey! No touching allowed!"

Ellis tuned out the announcer and concentrated on his caterpillar. He tried to do what he'd learned from Tink and from Mrs. Puckett. Whatever you say—say it from your heart.

"You-have-to-climb-up-and-you-have-to-climb-fast," he insisted. He said it as if it was all one word. He said it with energy and excitement and urgency.

Belle got it. She climbed. She never stopped. Not once.

The crowd screamed, "Go Zigzag! Go Dr. Pepper! Go Belle!"

Ellis heard Alice and Molly chanting, "You-can-do-it-you-can-do-it-you-can-you-can!"

"Belle is still in the lead, folks," said the man with the microphone. "Look at her go! What stamina. What persistence! And we have a winner! It's beautiful Belle by a mile!"

Ellis couldn't believe it. They'd won!

He wanted to hug Belle, but she was so far up the string he couldn't reach her. A seven-foot-tall man reached up and plucked her off. He was the official worm-remover, because nobody else could reach them.

"Congratulations!" he said.

"Thanks," said Ellis. He kissed Belle on the top of her prickly head. "You were great," he said. He looked for a head bob, but all he saw were her sides expanding out, then in. Out of breath.

Microphone Man hurried over, "Let's hear it for Ellis Coffey!" he shouted. He handed Ellis twenty-five dollars.

The crowd cheered again.

"Thank you," said Ellis.

"*You,*" cried Microphone Man, "have qualified for the last semifinal race! It's coming up next. Take your caterpillar to the nurse's station, then get yourself right back here for the next race. And hurry! You've got five minutes."

Ellis ran to the nurse's station. That's where all the winning worms were checked for steroids. He knew it was a joke—just part of the fun—but he was nervous anyway.

He stretched Belle out on a tiny hospital bed the size of

a matchbox. She was breathing easier now. A lady dressed like a nurse poked her gently a couple of times, then pretended to get a urine sample.

"She's clean," said the lady.

Ellis sighed in relief, thanked her, and ran back to the stage. On the way, dozens of people slapped him on the back and said, "Way to go!" "Good luck!" and "Go for the gold!"

Even Randy gave him a high-five.

He looked for Alice and Molly and George. They were waiting for him by the steps to the stage, looking at him like he was Superman.

Everything was happening so fast. Where were Mom and Dad? Did they know he'd won? Where had he put his twenty-five-dollar prize? What lane was he supposed to be in?

He opened his palm and looked at Belle. She was curled up in a ball. The other winners had gotten to rest between heats. Maybe Belle was tired. Was she resting?

"Hey," said Ellis. "Are you okay?"

Belle ignored him.

Had he accidentally squashed her?

"Ellis to Belle," he whispered. "Do you read me? Do you copy?"

Belle didn't move. Not even a twitch.

20   POOPED?

Was Belle okay? Ellis didn't know. She was still curled up in a ball. He looked to see if she was breathing. He couldn't tell.

"Belle?" he whispered.

Nothing.

He stroked her fuzz. He blew on her. He listened for caterpillar breaths, burps, hiccups . . . anything.

"Good luck, Ellis," Miss Bluford called to him. She was facing lane seven with Amazing Grace. Ellis stood in front of lane eleven.

"Thanks," he answered. "Good luck to you too!"

Ellis thought Belle was going to need more than luck. Right now she looked as if she needed a heart transplant or a blood transfusion. Maybe both.

Was she tired? Sick?

Ellis raised her close to his mouth and sang softly, "This little light of mine, I'm gonna let it shine."

Nothing.

Ellis figured Belle must have different favorite songs than Tink. "She'll Be Coming 'Round the Mountain"? "Itsy Bitsy Spider"? Maybe she didn't even like music. Whatever it was, he didn't have time to find out.

He wasn't even sure she was alive.

Ellis stroked her fuzz. "I *really* need you to win," he pleaded. "Dad needs you to win. You can do it, I know you can. Please wake up. Now. Now would be good. You would really like my dad. He—"

Belle uncurled slowly. Her whole body stretched like a yawn. She raised half of herself up and reached out toward the string.

Ellis wanted to shout, "Yes!" But he stayed calm.

"On your mark!" boomed the man with the mike. "Get set!"

Ellis placed Belle on her string. She grabbed hold.

"Go!"

Ellis released her. She took off even faster than before. Steady. Speedy. Sure.

"Belle has taken the lead!" shouted the man with the mike. "That worm's the belle of the ball! But, wait!

Amazing Grace is close behind. King Tut's bowing to the crowd, but he's not moving up! And here comes Super Snake!"

Belle was winning. Ellis knew he should feel great. But he didn't. Something wasn't right. She was racing up, and she was racing up fast. But still . . . Ellis sensed something slow, something sluggish.

Belle stopped. She didn't move at all. Not a hair. All her tiny feet were frozen in place.

"Go, go, go. You've got to run up, and you've got to run fast!"

She sat there.

"Belle has hit the wall, folks. But Super Snake is coming on strong! And King Tut's out of the gate!"

"Come *on*!" Ellis urged. "Now! Fast! Run! Win! You're amazing. Go, go, go!"

Belle swiveled her head toward Ellis. Her face seemed expressive, even through the fuzz. She was tossing him an annoyed, over-the-shoulder kind of look, as if she was telling him to back off because she had something better to do.

"No way!" cried Ellis. "Not now! *Nothing* is more important right now than getting to the top of this string. What's the matter with you?"

Whoa, thought Ellis. Get a grip. Calm down. Be supportive. Worm whisperers don't panic.

And then he saw the problem—the tip end of frass.

Belle was pooping.

"Super Snake has turned around!" boomed the loudspeaker. "He's going backward. Belle's taking a nap. King Tut's moving up. He's halfway home! B-Bear is gaining on him."

And Belle is pooping. Ellis thanked God that no one could see it but him.

"It's okay," he whispered in his most sympathetic voice. "Everybody poops. You can't help it. But could you hurry? Please? Maybe just speed it up a little?"

Belle took her time.

"Five racers are two feet from the finish!" shouted Microphone Man. "Six are still at the starting line. Two are going backward! Three are resting. Who's it gonna be, folks? Super Snake, B-Bear, or King Tut? Wait! Here comes Amazing Grace."

Ellis's insides were doing jumping jacks, but he pretended to be calm. He kept saying nice things, supportive things, encouraging things.

Finally, Belle pushed out the frass. Then she rippled her body as if she was flexing all her muscles. *Whoosh*—she spurted forward like water shooting out of a fountain.

"Would you look at that!" yelled Microphone Man. "Belle's climbing. She's climbing fast. Just look at that worm power!"

"Run-up-run-fast-run-up-run-fast-run-up-run-fast," Ellis urged. "For-Dad-for-Dad-for-Dad-for-Dad."

"Belle just passed Amazing Grace! She's zooming past B-Bear and Super Snake! She's gaining on King Tut! Wait, B-Bear has shifted into high gear. It's a three-worm race, folks! Who's it gonna be? King Tut, B-Bear, or Belle? Only one will go to the finals!"

"Belle-Belle-Belle," Ellis chanted. "Go-go-go!"

"And we haaaaaave a winner!" shouted Microphone Man. "It's Belle by a nose, with King Tut and B-Bear barely a hair behind!"

The crowd cheered. Microphone Man clapped. Ellis

hugged Belle with his pinky finger. She wrapped herself around it and hugged him back. "You won!" he tried to whisper, but it came out kind of loud, "You won!"

Ellis could hear Mom and Dad shouting. Ellis grinned—they *had* seen the race! Mom, Dad, Alice, and everyone he knew was shouting, "You won! Ellis, you won!"

The man with the worms on his hat handed him fifty dollars.

"The final race will begin in ten minutes!" announced the loudspeaker.

"One more time," Ellis whispered to Belle. "You only have to win one more time."

21 NOSE TO NOSE

Everyone that Ellis knew was slapping him on the back, shouting congratulations, yelling, "Way to go, Ellis!"

Mr. Turnmire was there, and so was Miss Bluford, who didn't seem to mind that Belle had beaten Amazing Grace. Dad had his arm around Mom, and they both looked proud enough to pop.

Alice, George, Molly, Mrs. Puckett, Doc Swenson, Mr. V, the mayor, Aunt Glory, Mrs. Paisley, the postmaster—everybody was all over Ellis, covering him up with "Wow!" and "Well done!" and "Way to go!"

Even Randy said, "That was awesome. How'd you do that?"

Ellis shrugged. How *had* he done it? Skill? Luck? Magic? Who cared? Ellis held Belle up in the air for everyone to see. The crowd cheered. Belle raced over his hand, across his wrist, past his elbow and up under his sleeve.

"This is it!" blared the loudspeaker. "The finals! The ultimate battle! A fight to the finish! Who's going to forecast our winter weather? Who's going to take home a thousand dollars?"

A thousand dollars.

The reality of it all hit Ellis like a lightning bolt. That's why he was here. To win a thousand dollars. He was one step away from giving Dad and Mom their life back.

He plucked Belle out from under her hiding place, placed her in his palm, and whispered, "You can do this."

She bobbed her head.

He looked at Mom and Dad. They hadn't looked this happy in months. He couldn't wait to tell them his plans for the prize money!

One back surgery, coming up!

"The final race, coming up!" announced the loudspeaker.

Ellis's stomach tightened into a knot the size of Miss Bluford's dog.

"Are the contestants ready?" asked Microphone Man.

Ellis nodded.

The other semifinal winners nodded.

Ellis appraised the competition: a farmer wearing bib overalls, a lady wearing a floppy hat and high heels, a high school guy with a lizard tattoo, and three kids about the same age as Ellis. One of them, a girl with pigtails, was in the lane closest to Ellis. The sign above her worm said Prince Hairy.

Ellis eyed all the woolly worms.

None of them looked as eager as Belle.

Ellis held Belle so close to his face that they touched. "You're the best," he whispered.

She did a hiccup move that tickled his nose. Ellis got a prickly sensation. He stuck his other hand under his nose and pressed hard to make the tickle go away. He didn't want to sneeze her off the stage.

"On your marks."

Ellis held her close to the string. He could feel her body rippling beneath his fingers, ready to race.

"Get set."

He placed her on the string.

"Go!"

He whipped his hand away.

"Belle is off and running!" shouted Microphone Man. "So is Prince Hairy! Rip Van Wrinkle is asleep, and Houdini is hanging upside down."

Ellis looked at Belle. She was moving up. She was moving fast! He didn't need violets—he was a worm whisperer!

"It's Belle and Prince Hairy! A royal battle. They're neck and neck, folks! Look at them go! They've left the rest of the field in the dust!"

Prince Hairy was moving just as fast as Belle.

Ellis felt as if he and the girl with pigtails were the only ones on the stage. No one else was close. It was a two-worm race.

"Go girl," he urged. "Faster, faster, faster!"

Belle stopped and looked at him.

"Prince Hairy has taken the lead!"

"Don't stop now!" screamed Ellis.

No, no, no, he warned himself. Don't yell. Be calm. "You can do it," he urged, soft but firm. "You're good. You're the best."

Belle twisted in mid-air, then dangled upside down.

"Belle's wavering. Houdini is beginning to move. Prince Hairy is headed up, up, and awaaaaaaaay!"

Ellis stared. Belle was still hanging upside down, frozen to her spot. She looked like an icicle, but fuzzy.

Ellis took a deep breath. "You've got to run up, and you've got to run fast. Do *not* give up!"

Belle curved herself up, gripped the string, and began to climb again.

"Prince Hairy's ahead by three lengths, but wait a minute, folks! Would you look at this? Belle is closing the gap! No one else is even close."

Ellis talked so fast it wasn't words anymore, just sounds. Soothing urges. Supportive pleas. Prayers.

The crowd roared.

Ellis sucked in a gasping breath—he'd forgotten to breathe. But it was okay—Belle was climbing.

"It's gonna be close!" shouted Microphone Man. "They're neck and neck! Nose and nose. Fuzzy to fuzzy! Look at them go!"

Ellis's heart was pounding so hard it felt as if it would jump out of his chest.

"We haaaaaaaave a winner!"

He shouted out a name. The roaring sound in Ellis's ears was so loud he couldn't hear. Was it crowd noise or blood rushing into his head?

What did he say?

"Prince Hairy's the winner!"

Prince Hairy? Did he say Prince Hairy? The girl next to Ellis was jumping up and down.

"What a race, folks! Belle's a fighter, but Prince Hairy has prevailed."

Prevailed? What did *prevail* mean?

But Ellis didn't need a definition. One look at Mom's face, and Dad's and Alice's and George's and Molly's, and he knew exactly what it meant.

It meant he'd lost.

22 🐛 A CURE

Mom wrapped Ellis in a hug and called him "Ellie baby." Dad advised him to "shake it off." Alice offered to share a funnel cake. Miss Bluford held Grace up to lick him. Mrs. Puckett soothed him with gentle, wise words. Randy told him second place wasn't bad.

George, Molly, Doc, Mr. V, Aunt Glory—*everybody* had a cure for losing. What Ellis needed was a cure for Dad.

He trudged down to the park while the mayor of Banner Elk read the winning woolly worm. Who cared what the winter weather forecast would be?

Alice, George, and Molly walked with him.

It felt nice to have friends. It felt awful to lose.

Unless Ellis robbed a bank, he'd never have a thousand dollars.

"You did everything you could," said Molly.

"Yeah," said George.

"Wait!" cried Alice. She pulled out the worm money. She sat down on a bench and counted it. "Fifty-five dollars!" she cried. "Ellis. How much have you got?"

He dug into his front pockets and found a fifty-dollar bill from winning the semifinal race and Doc's five dollars. But where was the twenty-five from the first heat? Had he lost it? He tried his back pocket. There it was.

George counted on his fingers and exclaimed, "You have one hundred and thirty-five dollars!"

"But the worm money's yours," said Ellis, waving his hand to include all of them.

"We want your dad to have it," said Molly.

George and Alice nodded in agreement.

"Thanks," answered Ellis, "but it's not enough." Besides, Ellis knew his dad. He'd never take their money.

Ellis handed Belle to Alice.

"Thanks," said Alice, "but we should let her go."

"Yeah," said Ellis, "I know."

Alice placed Belle on a rock and watched her crawl around. They all stared at her. Nobody said anything. What was there to say?

"You guys split the worm money three ways," said Ellis. "You found the worms."

175

"But you sold them," said Molly. "Let's divide it four ways."

"Fifty-five divided by four," muttered George and counted on his fingers again. Everyone waited. "I need a calculator," he said finally.

They all scrunched up their faces and tried to do the math in their heads. The best they could agree on was that four went into fifty-five thirteen times—with something left over.

"So," said Molly. "We each take thirteen dollars. With what's left, we buy a funnel cake and share it."

"Perfect," said Alice.

Ellis added up all his money. He had a total of ninety-three dollars that was all his. He took a dollar and placed it beside Belle on the rock.

"Of course!" cried Molly. "Belle should definitely get paid. She worked harder than anybody!"

"What'll she do with it?" wondered George.

"Buy violets," answered Ellis, "and a really big Porta-Potty."

They laughed.

Ellis sighed and got ready to tell Belle good-bye. "She needs to go spin a cocoon and turn into a butterfly."

"She hibernates," said Alice.

"Huh?"

"Woolly worms," said Alice, "spend the winter as larvae. They bury themselves in dark logs or under leaf litter when it starts to get cold. In the spring, she'll become an Isabella tiger moth."

"No kidding?"

Alice nodded.

Then he studied Belle with extra interest. "A tiger moth."

"An *Isabella* tiger moth," said Alice.

"Cool," said Ellis.

Belle did a perfect hiccup head bob that seemed to say "all done here" and began to crawl away.

Ellis stroked her fuzzy coat one more time, then watched her go. "Thanks," he said.

Alice waved.

Molly threw her a kiss.

Belle rippled her body.

"You forgot your money!" called George.

They watched her twitch a shoulder shrug, then disappear under some leaves. They all looked at the money, then at each other.

Ellis knew it would be dumb to leave perfectly good money on a rock at the park, but he couldn't make himself take it.

"Don't be stupid," said George. He picked up the dollar bill and stuffed it in Ellis's shirt pocket.

When they got back to the Festival, Mom and Dad were packing up the booth. Ellis helped them stack their empty boxes.

"We sold out of everything!" cried Mom. She pushed the straggly hairs away from her face and grinned. She looked exhausted but happy.

Dad's eyes had that pinched look they got when he hurt.

"Go on," he said to Ellis. "Hang out with your friends." He pointed to Alice, George, and Molly, who were hanging around the outside of the tent, waiting for Ellis.

"Nope," said Ellis. "I'll carry stuff to the truck." He waved his friends away. "I'll catch you later," he called.

They hesitated, but Ellis turned and began to work. When he looked back again, they were gone.

Dad took the cash box, climbed into his Jeep, and headed for home—to his recliner, his crossword, his trout flies, and his pain.

All the way home, Mom tried to cheer Ellis up.

"You didn't lose!" she said. "You won! You won two races. And a lot of money!"

Ellis nodded.

"I'm proud of you!"

Ellis shrugged.

"It was all so exciting, so much fun!"

"But, I wanted to win a thousand dollars," mumbled Ellis.

"Well, of course," said Mom. She laughed. "We *all* want to win a thousand dollars. But I may have some news for you that's just as good."

"Is Dad's back better?" asked Ellis.

"Well, no. It's not."

Then there wasn't any news that was better than winning a thousand dollars. Ellis turned to look out the window and count mailboxes.

179

* * *

At home, Dad wasn't in his recliner. He was standing by the kitchen door, waiting for them. He was smiling.

Mom looked at him expectantly.

He nodded.

She flew into his arms and they hugged each other like they'd been apart for five years instead of fifty minutes.

Ellis stared at them. "What's going on?"

"Sit," said Dad. He motioned for them to sit down at the kitchen table. The cash box sat in the middle of it, covering one of the cracks in the Formica top.

"You counted our profits?" asked Mom.

Dad nodded.

"How much."

"One thousand, seven hundred, and fifty-two dollars," he announced.

Mom let out a whoop.

Ellis stared at her.

"Does this mean—?"

"Yes," she said, squeezing Ellis's arm. "It means we can afford your Dad's surgery, with money left over."

Was she kidding?

"And we could never have done it without you," said Mom squeezing his arm even harder.

Dad nodded and slapped Ellis on the back.

"Huh?"

"Ellie baby," said Mom, "you helped make everything we sold. The jam, the bread, the pies. You picked all the blueberries. You did all the chores."

They both looked at him, wearing stupid grins and acting as if they might giggle or something.

He *had* done it. He, Ellis Coffey, had gotten a thousand dollars for his dad, and he hadn't even known he was doing it.

23 A SECRET FOR SPRING

The woolly worm on the big screen of their new TV looked a lot like Belle, except that it was frozen solid. The narrator explained that's what happens to a woolly worm when it hibernates. Its heart stops beating, then its gut freezes, and then its blood.

"Whoa," said Ellis. "Why doesn't it die?"

"Don't know," answered Dad. He was sitting up straight in his chair, completely recovered from his surgery.

"It survives," said the TV narrator, "by producing a cryoprotectant in its tissues."

"A what?" said Ellis.

"Cryo-something," said Dad.

"Push Replay," said Ellis.

Dad fumbled around for a minute, searching for the right button, then he pushed it.

"By producing a cryoprotectant," repeated the narrator.

Ellis grabbed a pencil and paper off the coffee table and wrote down *crioprotektent* and hoped that he was spelling it right. "Mr. Turnmire will love this," he said.

Then the TV footage advanced from winter to spring. Ellis watched the caterpillar thaw and then pupate and emerge as an Isabella tiger moth. It had soft yellow wings with little black spots like someone had randomly splattered a few tiny drops of ink on it. Ellis thought it was beautiful.

Dad pointed the remote at the TV and clicked it off. "Just think," he said. "Belle is going to do that."

"Yeah," said Ellis, grinning. He was glad he and Alice had let Belle go.

But Ellis was happy for another reason; and not just because Dad had gotten his surgery and Mom found a new job with better hours and they had a new TV.

Ellis had a secret that he'd only told to Alice and George and Molly.

Something amazing had happened a week after the Woolly Worm Festival. Ellis had reached under his bed hoping to find his shoes. Instead, he found the old shoe box that Tink had lived in. Seeing it made him sad, so he threw it in the trash can. When her spongy stick spilled out, he picked it up and looked at it.

Two black beads stared back.

It was Tink!

Ellis couldn't believe it!

"Tink! You're not dead!"

He worm-whispered every thing he could think of.

"Come out!"

"I missed you!"

"Are you okay?"